RICHARD

MURDER
AT THE
Craft Show

Richard Baldwin

Published by Buttonwood Press, LLC

P.O. Box 716, Haslett, Michigan 48840

www.buttonwoodpress.com

DISCLAIMER:

This novel is a product of the author's imagination. The events described in this story never occurred. Though localities, buildings, and businesses may exist, liberties were taken with their actual locations and descriptions. This story has no purpose other than to entertain the reader.

ISBN 978-9998096-1-7
Printed in the USA

Cover photo credits:
Plaque: andreykuzmin © 123RF.com
Craftshow: The Chamber of Commerce Grand Haven, Spring Lake, Ferrysburg

Published by Buttonwood Press, LLC
P.O. Box 716, Haslett, Michigan 48840
www.buttonwoodpress.com

Dedication

This book is dedicated to fellow crafter, Jerry Neikirk, who suggested this book. Whenever he saw me over a period of years, he would ask, "How's 'Murder at the Craft Show' coming?" I would usually respond with, "Thinking about it, Jerry." Finally, through his perseverance, the pen began to move over the paper resulting in this story. Thanks, Jerry, for keeping your goal in mind and prodding me to move. This is dedicated to you, my friend.

Other Mysteries by Richard L. Baldwin

Acknowledgements

There are many people whose talents and skills contributed to this story. I thank my publication team: Editor Anne Ordiway, Proofreader, Joyce Wagner; cover designer and typesetter, Marie Kar; and printer, Bonnie Kahler of Data Reproductions.

Others who provided assistance with research include: David Kirk, Chief of Police for St. John's Michigan; Ed Kaiser; and Jerry and Nancy Neikirk,

There are others from the Buttonwood Press team to acknowledge: Vivian Fahle, Manager; Jennifer Thompson, Bookkeeper; Sandra Bieber, Sales Representative; From the sidelines you are invaluable.

Finally, I am eternally indebted to my wife Carol (Patty) Baldwin for her support, encouragement and belief in me. You are the GREATEST.

Prologue

Craft shows are unique. They are as American as apple pie and Chevrolet. Such an event is a collection of people who seem to have found their niche, whether as a career or as a hobby.

In addition to being extremely creative, crafters are friendly, courteous, and almost always willing to help another, be it putting up a tent—covering, hauling a heavy box, or answering a question. These would-be-vagabonds meet on weekends and renew friendships or acquaintances while hoping to encounter buyers—not just lookers.

However, a few things most, if not all, crafters know are sacred; not sacred in a religious sense, but in the sense of etiquette. The most common example is turf. Each vendor 'rents' a space in a venue, usually 10'x10' or 12'X12'. The promoter usually marks the space with tape, paint, or chalk. So, for forty dollars to hundreds of dollars, the vendor knows that this is "home" and going into the space of another is not acceptable. That just isn't done, or if it is, it shouldn't be.

Another unspoken rule is hawking beyond one's booth. Sometimes a worker from a booth will approach people walking in aisles and hand them a flyer or invite them to visit his or her booth. This draws attention away from nearby booths which is not seen as positive. This also applies to vendors making music or "noise", anything that gives one vendor an edge when it comes to seeking attention from possible customers.

Finally, some vendors put signs in areas outside their assigned spaces. Once again, it is taking an advantage unfair to other crafters. Up is okay. Flags, banners, signs atop poles from the canopy are fine. The rented space is understood to go Up but not Out.

Sometimes disturbances occur outside of the crafter's control. For example, friends, relatives, or neighbors gather in front of a booth to visit. This can take anywhere from a few minutes to several minutes and again, it doesn't allow fair opportunity for guests to see all the offerings.

It is with this understanding of the "rules" of etiquette that this story unfolds.

Chapter ONE

There was tension at the Farmington Hills Park, site of the Annual Craft Show sponsored by the Chamber of Commerce. The day was exceptionally hot and a mid-July heat wave can make people and events difficult. If it is too hot, customers stay away, sales will be down, and vendors are confined to their booths. Those with electricity may set up a small fan. Drinking water is critical to prevent dehydration.

Vendor Cory Becker was visibly upset—pacing and looking quite perturbed. He continually shook his head from side to side, and anyone looking at him could tell something was bothering him.

Cory was a veteran crafter. His specialty was high-quality pens, wine bottle stoppers, and ice cream scoops. He was 63 years of age and blessed with a full head of hair. He dressed fashionably because he felt that he and his products needed to ooze quality and craftsmanship.

Judy Gentillozi, a nearby crafter, was angered because her friend, Cory, was so upset. She hoped a heart attack was not imminent. There was a lull in traffic at her booth so she approached Cory. "What's bothering you, my friend?"

"I hate doing a show when Stan Fedewa is here. He undercuts me in selling his wares, which by the way are similar to mine. He strolls through the crowd passing out flyers, promising to beat anybody's price by up to 50%. I can't compete with him around."

"I hope you complained to the show director?" Judy asked.

"I mentioned it, but Fedewa still does it. This show director is about as helpful as sand in a desert."

"Have you talked to Fedewa about your concern?"

"Oh, yeah. He always says, 'It's America, pal. It's capitalism. It's competition. You can't fault me for wanting to sell my product.'"

"I told him in no uncertain terms, 'You're not fair to other vendors who play by the rules, who don't undercut competition, and who don't advertise beyond their booth space'. He got angry —some might say, threatening. He told me, 'Get a life! Get with the program!' Words like that."

"Well, it's not right," Judy agreed. "Who mans his booth when he's out promoting his wares?"

"Some woman," Cory replied. "I don't know her. She might be a relative, a neighbor, or a friend. She's worked with him at a few other shows, but I never asked her name."

"Let karma take care of it," Judy suggested. "His bad behavior will come back to bite him at some time."

"Yeah, but in the meantime, I'm not even making my booth fee," Cory said again, shaking his head. "I even had one customer say to me, 'How can you compete with that guy? He's ripping you off. Do something! Knock him off.'"

"Knock him off?" I asked.

"I don't mean kill him, but do something to fight back."

"Like what?" I asked.

"She suggested, 'Carry a placard that says, 'Fedewa's not fair to vendors. Don't give your money to a crook!'"

"I replied, 'The manager won't go along with that.'"

"'Then forget the manager,' she said. 'If he confronts you, threaten him in some way.'"

"It's not in my personality. I'll just pack up and leave. I'll complain to others, like you, or get angry, but I won't take matters into my own hands. Thanks for being supportive."

"Then she said, 'If you won't do anything, I just might. This is wrong, quite unfair, and it gives this show a black eye.'"

"I told her to do what she wanted, but don't pull me into it."

Judy asked, "Who was that customer?"

"I don't know her name but she has bought from me before. She was upset, I noted a serious tone to her voice. She smiled as she said, 'nobody messes with my favorite vendor! I don't like him or what he's doing to you. Somebody's got to do something, and that somebody just might be ME!'"

Before leaving the Farmington Hills show, Cory let Stanley have a piece of his mind as he did earlier in the day. He left with a pointed finger and a raised voice, "Shame on you!"

The manager approached Cory and reprimanded him for leaving early, a clear violation of show rules.

"Yeah, well what about Fedewa?" Cory barked. "He doesn't follow your rules! What are you going to do about him?" The manager walked away realizing Cory was right.

Cory's vendor friends were most sympathetic and helped him take down his booth and display items. Judy said, "See you at the next show. You are a good man, Cory. We're sorry you were treated so poorly not only by Stan but by the show's management."

Cory thanked his friends for their understanding and their help. He got in his packed van and left the craft show area.

Vendors arrived at the park early to set up and prepare for the second day of the show. The show area came alive with vendors working, people walking to and from the hospitality tent where free coffee and donuts were available.

While in the hospitality tent, Johnny Facely asked to speak to the manager. Vicki Kaiser came out and greeted Johnny. "I don't know if you know it, but the show is soon to open and Booth #42 has not opened."

Vicki looked at her clip board which contained a map of the

show grounds and the names of the vendors. "Oh, that's Stanley Fedewa's booth. He's never on time. We've just come to accept each vendor and their idiosyncrasies. I'll check on him in a few minutes. Thanks for telling me."

About a half-hour into the show Ed Kaiser, a vendor selling his humor books in the area of Stan's booth, became curious. He wandered over to the enclosed booth. First he shouted, "Hey, Stan, are you in there?" There was no response.

Ed reached down at one of the corners and pulled up the zippered booth flap. At first he didn't see anything. But, when he looked down, he saw Stan lying in a pool of blood, looking quite dead. Startled, Ed did not call 911, nor did he say a word to anyone. He zipped the booth closed and prepared to leave hoping nobody saw him. But, afraid that someone may have seen him opening and closing the booth, he returned to his booth walking behind a row of crafters.

About an hour into the show, Vicki, the show's director, found Stan's booth enclosed in white fabric. She reached down and pulled up the zipper. She immediately saw Stanley lying in blood. Unlike Ed she used her audio phone to call Security and 911. She then got the attention of several vendors in the area. She told them, "We have a medical emergency here. Police and paramedics will arrive shortly."

"Is he dead?" a vendor asked. Vicky thought it odd that the vendor mentioned death. There was no way for others to see what she saw in the booth.

Vicki simply said, "Someone needs medical attention, and the police will want to interview each of you. You can close up your booths, and perhaps reopen after the police leave, or I have some spots a distance down this walkway where you can set up. It's up to you. If you decide to move, please vacate the area quickly as the paramedics and police will rope off the area as soon as they arrive."

None of the vendors wanted to move. As directed. they closed their booths and stood back to watch the police carry out their responsibilities. Sirens could be heard approaching. Volunteers at the gate directed the vehicles to the scene and assisted police in keeping the ever-increasing crowd back.

Three uniformed paramedics with bags and a gurney arrived first. They entered the booth and pulled the zipper down for privacy. It was obvious to them that the male victim was dead, so no resuscitation procedures were employed. One of the paramedics talked to the Medical Examiner on the phone. The ME was on the way to the park.

The paramedics reported to the police chief who directed a detective and photographer to enter the tent. At the same time, the police cordoned off the scene with yellow crime tape. Curious people stood behind the yellow tape watching, wondering, and talking.

Newspaper and TV reporters were on the scene questioning witnesses and authorities.

Chapter TWO

The victim was 61-year-old Stanley Fedewa. When he wasn't hawking his pens, Stan had been a groundskeeper at a fashionable golf course in Oakland County. Stan was a confirmed bachelor, had enjoyed friendships with women, but his difficult personality caused women to leave before they considered a serious relationship.

Stan resembled a professional wrestler except for his protruding belly. He had a beard that was not well groomed.

Everything in Stan's life was about him. There was no room in his life for other people and their needs. He was a control freak. Every dollar was spent for a purpose, and that was to fulfill one of his dreams. It was far out of character, but he drove an expensive foreign car, and he was often smoking a cigar even where no smoking was the law.

Detective Russ Wheeler removed the wallet from the victim's back pocket. He noted the name, data on the driver's license, and put the wallet in an evidence bag. Other pants pockets yielded change and a money clip containing several hundred-dollar bills. The detective also found a receipt for a bar that hosted Texas Hold'em tournaments.

The medical examiner arrived, certified death, and authorized the removal of the body to the county morgue. Cause of death appeared to be repeated stabbing in the chest. A wire was found near the body and there was a circular bruise that cut into the skin around the neck.

No one was allowed inside a roped-off area that included two or three booth spaces. The police photographer took multiple photos of the body sprawled on the ground in a pool of blood.

After photographs were complete, the body was placed in a body bag, lifted onto the gurney, and then rolled to the ambulance. People gawked as the gurney passed, wondering who was on the stretcher or how death came to the person.

Next, the forensic team entered the enclosed booth and scoured the 10-foot by 10-foot space and surrounding area for clues. The murder was thought to have occurred in the booth. There was no sign of a struggle so the detective theorized that the killer had been in the tent when Stan entered, either late at night or well before other vendors came to the show grounds.

After two hours of investigation, the booth and everything inside was removed and taken away. It was time for the show to attempt some normalcy for the remainder of the day. People were allowed to move in the area.

✂

At home in Royal Oak, Cory Becker turned on his television. He saw the word Bulletin and heard an announcer say, "A murder has occurred at the Farmington Hills Craft Show. A vendor at the show was apparently attacked in his booth sometime during the night. No suspects have been identified. Apparently there were no witnesses. The victim's name has not been released. The show was closed for a few hours this morning, but it reopened around eleven. The show director has urged people to attend the show, noting that it is safe to do so. We will have more information as it becomes available. Reporting from Farmington Hills, Philip Watson, TV 4 News."

Cory knew instantly that the dead vendor must be Stan Fedewa and he knew that his vendor friends would think that he killed him. He turned off the television and called his wife Nancy, who was out shopping, and answered his call in Kroger's.

"Stan Fedewa has been murdered at the craft show," Cory began.

"The guy you were upset with?" Nancy asked.

"That's him."

"Where was he murdered?"

"The TV bulletin says he was killed in his booth."

"Do they know who did it?" Nancy asked, afraid of what she would hear.

"Police have no witnesses or suspects at this time. But, I know who the main suspect is…"

"You."

"Exactly. I was mad at him, expressed it, and would be the most logical person to want him killed, because I DID want him dead."

"Have you heard from the police or media?"

"Not yet. I called you first. What should I do?" Cory asked. "Call the police? Call our lawyer? Call our daughter?"

"I'm coming right home," Nancy replied in a concerned voice. "You need support. This is stressful and will remain so."

Cory called his lawyer, Norm Sawyer. His advice was to say nothing to anyone. He would arrive at the Becker home and soon would handle everything.

"Should I call the police to declare my innocence right off the bat?" Cory asked Norm.

"No. Wait for me to arrive."

"But, wouldn't it be in my best interests to contact the police immediately?"

"No, we'll discuss it when I get there."

At the craft show, detectives were busy interviewing vendors, customers, or anyone who may have heard or seen anything related to the crime.

The vendor next to Stan at first declined to be interviewed, but she changed her mind when she heard another vendor saying damning things about Stan and his conflict with Cory.

"Okay, okay, I'll make a statement," said the vendor who sold wind catchers.

"Thank you. I'll record this. What's your name?" a detective asked.

"Trudy Gonzales."

"Go ahead."

"Yes, there was an argument yesterday. My friend Cory Becker was frustrated and understandably so, because Fedewa was not being fair to Cory, or anyone in this area."

"What do you mean?" the detective asked.

"He was breaking show rules: undercutting vendors, advertising outside of his rented space, and promising a better product than his competitors at a much reduced price."

"So, this Cory was upset?"

"Of course; so was I and others."

"Who is the man you refer to as Cory?"

"His name is Cory Becker. He lives in Royal Oak. He didn't do this, Officer. I'm not implying that. In fact, I'm certain that violence is not possible with Cory. Mad, left angry, yes, but murder, or even violent contact is not in Cory's personality."

While the detective was taking information from Trudy, another detective was interviewing the show's manager, Vicki, who related the same information about the complaints and conflicts between Cory and Stan. A newspaper reporter was standing within earshot of the interview with Vicki, and upon hearing the name of the vendor set about finding him.

19

Within fifteen minutes, the police, Cory's wife Nancy, daughter Erin, a news crew, and a county sheriff had pulled up to the Becker home. But thankfully, the first person to arrive had been his lawyer, Norm Sawyer, who only lived a couple of blocks away. Nancy and Erin gave Cory hugs. Nancy had called their neighborhood watch to forestall rumors from circulating. The message to neighbors was, "A crime was committed at the Farmington Hills Craft Show, and the police are investigating those vendors in the vicinity, including Cory. Sorry about all of this excitement. It's routine procedure. The vehicles should be gone soon."

Nancy started the phone tree and the message spread throughout the subdivision. Some neighbors stood around gawking, wondering and questioning.

The police along with the deputy sheriff, congregated in the living room. The drapes were drawn. The Farmington Hills Police Department led the investigation. The newspaper reporter and film crew remained on the sidewalk. Mr. Sawyer was very cautious that Cory didn't blurt out something innocent that could be taken as incriminating.

The police began questioning by saying to Cory, "We understand you had an argument with the victim yesterday. True?"

"Yes. True. He was not following craft show rules and he was undercut…"

"That's enough," interrupted Mr. Sawyer. "Yes, they argued, but my client was simply doing what any person would do in a similar situation."

The police continued. "Voices were raised, accusations made, fingers were pointed. The confrontation was disturbing, yes?"

"Yes," Cory said.

"You felt so strongly about what this man was doing that you sought out the show director and complained?"

"Yes, I sure did. I paid for my booth space, and I should have a fair chance to sell my wares without being hassled by that jerk," Cory said with voice rising.

Again, lawyer Sawyer cut into the conversation. "My client was following correct protocol. He approached the manager of the show to express his displeasure at Mr. Fedewa's behavior."

"Where were you last evening?" the detective asked. "Let's begin with leaving the show."

"I drove to Art's Bar," Cory began. "I wanted a beer to relax and calm my nerves a bit."

"One beer?" the detective asked.

"No, probably two or three."

"Then, where did you go?"

"Home."

Looking at Nancy and Erin, the officer said, "Were you home when Cory arrived?"

Each nodded negatively.

The detective turned to Cory, "Did you speak to a neighbor when you got home?"

"No."

"Did you stay home?"

"No, I went to play some golf."

"Where?"

"Rolling Hills Golf Club," Cory replied.

"Isn't that where the victim has maintenance responsibilities?"

"Yes."

"You went there to play or to confront Mr. Fedewa?"

"Well, I guess…"

Once again attorney Sawyer interrupted, "My client went to play golf. What else does one do at a golf course?" The police detective looked at the county sheriff and nodded ever so briefly. He then asked Cory, "Did you see Stan Fedewa while you were at the course?"

"Yes."

"Still angry?"

"I was still angry obviously, but I had cooled and didn't confront him."

"Did he confront you?"

Cory paused. The lawyer pulled him aside. "What happened at the course?" Norm asked.

"He threatened me."

"In what way?"

"He said my complaining got him in trouble with the show director and he was told not to return to the show now or ever, for that matter."

"So, you just listened and walked away?"

"No, I said something stupid."

"What did you say?"

"I said, 'I've had enough of your irresponsibility. You're a terrible human being!'"

"Then what happened?"

"We stared one another down but we didn't talk after that."

"So, you returned to playing golf?"

"Yes."

"Did he say what he was going to do?"

"He said he was going back to the craft show to dismantle his booth and remove his wares."

Cory and his lawyer returned to the gathering in the living room. "Where were we?" Mr. Sawyer asked.

"I asked your client what he did when he went to the golf course. Did he go to play golf or to confront the victim?"

"Yes, I recall," Norm Sawyer replied. "My client did interact with the victim. They had some words, and then my client played golf."

The detective turned to Cory. "Did the victim say what he was going to do after this confrontation?"

"My client pleads the fifth," Norm said quickly. If the police knew Stan said he was going back to his booth, Cory would have known where Stan would be, allowing the possibility that Cory could have followed him to the park.

The interview produced insufficient information to arrest Cory. The detective informed him that he would be questioned again the next day. Mr. Sawyer stated that his client would cooperate completely. "He has nothing to hide. Yes, he was angry as he had a right to be, but he did not murder this man."

The police vehicles finally pulled away, leaving the neighbors wondering what this was all about.

✂

A newspaper reporter found a neighbor more than willing to share his thoughts about Cory.

"What can you tell me about Mr. Becker personally?"

"Nice guy. He'd give you the shirt off his back."

"Does he have a mean streak?"

"I've never seen him out of control. A perfect neighbor if you ask me."

Once the authorities had left, Nancy, Erin, and Cory had a family hug. Nancy looked at Cory and said, "Who killed Fedewa?"

"I don't know," Cory replied. "Other vendors were not happy with him and were very supportive of me. No one in the craft world would kill another, no matter what was said or done. Whoever killed the guy is someone outside of the craft show."

"Dad, why do the police think you're involved?" Erin asked.

"I'm a suspect. I had a confrontation with him. I talked to him at the golf course. I can't provide the name of anyone who saw me in the early evening."

Erin was almost in tears. "You didn't kill this guy, did you, Dad?"

"No, I certainly did not," Cory reassured Erin. "People will think what they want and I'm sure rumors will circulate."

Chapter THREE

Lou Searing was no stranger to craft shows. They were his major means of offering his books to the public. Lou thought of his selling at craft shows as having a travelling bookstore.

Lou was not at the Farmington Hills show. He was in Houghton Lake participating in their craft show. He had just replenished his display table with more books when his phone rang. He did not recognize the caller, so he refused the call. Several potential buyers were at his booth and for Lou, customers deserve prompt service.

Ten minutes later his phone rang again and again he did not recognize the caller, but no customers were at his booth, so he picked up the phone.

"Hello. This is Lou Searing."

"Lou, this is a voice from your past."

"Well, I don't recognize your voice, so I've not a clue who you are."

"Jerry Neikirk from Nature's Design."

"Great to hear from you, Jerry. What's on your mind?"

"Have you ever heard of a crafter named Stan Fedewa?"

"Difficult guy," Lou said. "I was at a show with him once and I didn't get good vibes. I didn't like him, but I don't recall why—he just didn't seem like a nice guy. Quite stuck on himself."

"That's the guy. Well, he's dead."

"Okay. I'm sorry, I guess," Lou said matter-of-factly. "It's never a good thing to hear that someone dies. Heart attack?"

"Murdered in his booth," Jerry said.

"No way."

"I'm not pulling your leg. You know that I've wanted you to write a mystery titled 'Murder at the Craft Show' for years now."

"So, now you're giving me a real-life plot."

"I thought you might be a good one to solve it."

"Who is the suspect?"

"Ever heard of Cory Becker?"

"Oh, sure. He's the exact opposite of Fedewa. Cory has a heart of gold. Why's he a suspect?"

"He got into a shouting match with Fedewa the afternoon of the murder. There was bad blood between them. Cory was so mad at him that he took his booth down and left the show."

"Did Cory kill him?" Lou asked.

"He was pretty mad, Lou. It was scary."

"I'm sorry. It must have been a trying experience. Nobody should have to experience this."

"Are you going to investigate it?"

"I can't just jump in," Lou remarked. "There's protocol. The Farmington Hills Police have jurisdiction, I assume. If I investigate, it will be at the invitation of the responsible law enforcement agency."

"I see. Can I suggest to the police that you're available should they want some help?" Jerry asked.

"If I can help, sure."

"The Chief of Police, Lawrence Profit is in my Rotary Club. I'll mention it to him."

"I think you know that I'm interested, but I always want Carol's blessing before I saddle up and head off to unsafe territory."

"I wear the pants in my family as well," Jerry said, with a chuckle. "The problem is that's all I do, is wear the pants. I know who the alpha dog is and it isn't me."

Lou replied, "I'll talk with Carol and get back to you."

Lou and Carol and their pets, Sami the golden retriever and Sami II the cat, live in a home south of Grand Haven on the shore of Lake Michigan. Both Lou and Carol were beginning to slow down. Carol was approaching her 80th birthday and Lou was close behind at 77. Life in the fast lane was no longer their reality.

Carol was making a rhubarb sauce when Lou called. She hadn't expected him home from Houghton Lake because the show covered two days, and it made no sense to drive back and forth for overnight.

"How are sales going?" Carol asked, always interested in Lou's selling.

"I'm having a good show. I'm seeing some of my regulars and many new buyers. The weather is good and the crowds are heavy."

"That's good."

"Yeah, I'm blessed, that's for sure."

"I suppose you're calling to get my permission to investigate that murder I heard about down in Farmington Hills," Carol said, getting right to the point.

"How could you know about that?"

"The story is in the news. It's getting a lot of air time."

"Actually, I was calling about that. I respect your wishes—always have. If you will be upset if I get involved, I won't; plain and simple."

"Oh Lou, I appreciate your running it by me, but I'm pretty accepting of your work. What's this for you, case twenty or so?"

"Nineteen books, so yes, this would be my twentieth investigation, if the police want me and you approve."

"And you're still living to tell about it," Carol said.

"Pretty lucky guy, me."

"You go ahead and jump in; I'll alert the flower shop that keeping my spray of roses for your coffin is back on the front burner."

"Thanks for your support. When this show is over tomorrow afternoon, I'll head to Farmington Hills to begin investigating. But, as you know I will only get involved if I'm invited."

"Law enforcement loves you, Lou. They'll welcome you with open arms."

"So far, that has been the case, but there is always a first, and this could be it. Now, I've got a couple waiting to buy books, so I've got to go. I'll call this evening."

"Love you, Lou. Keep on having fun."

✂

Missing from the entire hubbub was the woman who had worked in Fedewa's booth. She never appeared at the show on day two. Some thought she was not scheduled to work the second day so there was no reason for her to appear.

The police detective found that, on the craft show application, a woman by the name of Becky Dawson was listed as a person to be working in the booth, but there was no address, phone number or email address for her. Becky was obviously a person of interest, and the fact that she didn't surface added to the belief that perhaps she was involved in the murder.

The forensic scientists assigned to the case found a number of fingerprints, but with the booth being visited by dozens of people provided little hope that someone's guilt could be determined through fingerprints. The prints were added to a file in case they appeared elsewhere.

The craft show photographer was asked to review all of his photographs in hopes of seeing Becky.

The morning paper appealed to anyone with information to come forward.

Lou called Jerry to see if he had learned anything about his being welcomed to the investigation. "The Chief will get back to me. He's heard of you and respects your work, but he isn't keen on bringing you in. It might reflect a lack of confidence in his team. But, this appears to be a difficult case with no suspects, weapon, or motive. I think he wants to go it alone. He was willing to share information and had no trouble with you getting involved, but it would be on behalf of a client. Stay tuned, I could be wrong."

"Okay. I understand."

"I have a call into Cory now," Jerry explained. "I'll ask him if he wants to hire you to investigate on his behalf."

"There's no fee. I write a book about each of my cases, and then I sell the books. That's all the thanks I need."

"I'll get back to you as soon as I talk to Cory."

Stan Fedewa's only living relative was a stepbrother in Minneapolis, but the two men appeared to be strangers. The man vaguely remembered Stan, but said he wouldn't recognize him if he knocked on his front door. Other than acknowledging the death, there was no remorse.

Chief Profit called Jerry and said he would welcome Lou and his skills. He also told Jerry he didn't think Cory needed a detective to work on his behalf because he thought him to be innocent. Jerry convinced Chief Prophet that an opportunity to get the talents of Lou Searing shouldn't be passed up. He apparently agreed. Within a minute, Jerry called Lou and said, "Chief Prophet welcomes Lou to his team."

"Guess I'll get right to work," Lou said, happy to get the news. "I'll come to Farmington Hills tomorrow evening to talk to Mr. Becker. Could you get me the names of the vendors who had booths in the area? I'll want to talk to them, in a group or privately. Skype, Facetime, or minimally a conference call would suffice."

Jerry did as asked and set up a conference call between the five vendors who were in the area of Stan's booth. Fortunately, two of the four knew Lou from past craft shows.

Lou began the conversation, "Well, this time we meet under a cloud. Our colleague, Stan Fedewa, has been murdered, and Chief Profit has asked me to assist in the investigation. I have been able to find out that the woman who worked in Stan's booth is vital to this investigation. Does anyone know her? Did anyone talk to her at the Farmington show or any other? Finding Becky Dawson is priority one."

Mike of the Mackinac Island Fudge booth began. "I've seen her at other shows. She's a loner. I've seen her waiting on customers but never talking leisurely with anyone. I thought she was Stan's daughter or a relative, but that's just a guess."

"Thanks, Mike. We know he has no family to speak of."

"I think I have a clue," began Michelle Bosecker, who sold soaps and healing concoctions. "I was playing golf at the course where Stan works when he recognized me. He pulled up in a golf cart with a young woman. I can't say with any certainty that she was Becky, but she fits the description. Her arms were covered with tattoos, anyway."

"Good observation, Michelle. It makes sense that he would ask one of his employees at the golf course to work his booth. I'll check the staff at the golf club."

Quiet till now, Bonnie, of leather belts, spoke up. "I've a theory. I sort of think outside the box, and my idea may be far-fetched, but I'll offer it, just the same."

"Any idea is welcome," Lou said. "So, Bonnie, let's hear it."

"Well, the murder took place inside an enclosed booth. If I was the murderer, I would want to be sure nobody was in the area to hear any commotion. So, I'm curious as to why the murder took place in the booth. It would make much more sense to kill him away from that area. Lou, you're the detective, but I don't understand why Stan was murdered in his booth."

Lou remarked, "That points to Becky. Stan would expect her to be at the booth. She could have asked him to return that night for some purpose."

Jane, a vendor of fine jewelry, spoke next. "It might not have been Becky who killed him. Or, she could have hired a hit man to do the job."

"Good point," Lou responded. "What surprises me is that Becky has not surfaced. The news has been widely broadcast, so one would think she would show up, even help with the investigation."

"Exactly," Mike added.

Sharon Dickinson, who specialized in doll clothes, listened, but she didn't contribute to the conversation.

Lou contacted Russ Wheeler, the Farmington Hills police detective, who was assigned to the case. The chief asked Russ to work with Lou, to consider him one of the team, without admitting that he had been brought on to help. Detective Wheeler, a veteran of the force, had a great deal of experience in investigating murders. Russ was physically fit, mid-thirties, and a family man.

"Was anything stolen from the booth?" Lou asked

"We found no evidence of that."

"Any signs of a struggle?"

"None. We suspect he was sitting at the table where the killer reached around from behind him, plunging the knife into his chest. We believe it was a quick attack. He didn't know what hit him, as the saying goes. Ironically, there was money on the table in front of Stan. It appeared that he was counting the day's take."

"It would have been easy for the murderer to take some money," Lou concluded. "Cash wasn't the reason for the killing, I guess."

Lou drove to the Rolling Hills Golf Course after arranging an interview with the manager, Roger Walsh. The two greeted each other cordially. "You're here to talk about Becky, I presume?" Roger asked.

"Yes, she has information we need. What can you tell me about her family, job, personality quirks?"

"Well, as I told the police earlier, Rebecca Dawson is a part-time employee in the course maintenance department."

"Address?"

"Our personnel manager tells me she lives at a shelter for abused women. I guess the shelter people are trying to find housing for her."

"What was her relationship with Stan Fedewa?"

"Stan's her boss. He has become a father figure to her. He tried to find odd jobs that gave her some money to add to her minimum-wage maintenance job."

"Have you seen her since the murder?" Lou asked.

"No. I did try to reach her at the shelter, but they said she had not come back that evening."

"Is that typical of her personality?"

"She's a free spirit," Roger admitted. "We suspect she has trouble with drugs. We think she hangs with undesirable folk."

"So, in a nutshell, nobody knows where she is," Lou summarized. "The police are looking for her, and so am I."

"I'll let you know if and when she shows up."

"Thanks. Oh, one more question, did she have a car?"

"Nope. She had a suspended license, can't get insurance, and couldn't make payments."

"Family?"

"Can't locate anyone."

"Thanks, I'll be in touch."

The police treated Becky as a missing person. Her name was placed in the missing persons file, meaning that she would be sought by criminal investigators all over the country.

✂

Lou called Carol to summarize the investigation and to tell her of his plans to come home. "Boy, I walked into a puzzle with this one."

"You love the challenge," Carol responded.

"Yes, I do, but I like a clue or two. So far I'm at a dead-end with little hope of finding something to investigate."

"You know ideas will surface, and you'll be off and running," Carol reminded Lou.

"I suppose you're right."

"When do you plan to come home?" Carol asked.

"Soon. I've been in touch with the police, and I've a list of contacts. In a day or two I'll be ready for one of our walks along the Lake Michigan shore."

"I hope so. The evenings are gorgeous right now. Hurry home so we can enjoy the sunsets and cool breezes."

"I'll be in touch. I wanted to let you know where I was and what was happening."

"Thanks. Love you, Lou."

That night, Lou stayed at the Comfort Inn in Farmington Hills. He was tired after a long show followed by a drive to Farmington Hills and working on a new case.

He was hungry so he went to Panera's and got a chocolate chip bagel with cream cheese and a cup of decaf coffee. The quiet and having time to relax felt good.

Lou's brain was being bombarded with thoughts of the murder and what he needed to do to solve it when the phone rang in his motel room. The ring startled him because as far as he knew, only Carol knew where he was. *Maybe it was the front desk calling with some information?* he thought.

"Hello." Silence.

"Hello. Who's this?" Lou asked again.

Silence and then Lou heard the phone click and a disconnect followed.

Lou thought, *I'm being stalked. Just what I need. I hate to always be looking over my shoulder.*

In time, he forgot about the interruption. He watched a ball game for about an hour, and then went to bed.

About 1:45 a.m., Lou was awakened by a rap on his door. Startled, he got out of bed, looked through the peep hole, but saw nothing. He went to the window and parted the curtains with great care, but he didn't see anyone. He had trouble getting back to sleep, but eventually he did. There were no interruptions for the rest of the night. Lou went to get his continental breakfast and coffee; nothing out of the ordinary happened.

Then Lou suspected damage might have been done to his car during the night. He checked out of his room, left a tip for the maid, and proceeded to the parking lot. He thought the worst, expecting slit tires or eggs thrown onto the car's surface, but the car seemed okay. He looked for someone sitting in a car watching his every move, but he saw no one.

Chapter FOUR

When Lou heard that Becky might be into drugs, he thought a drug deal gone bad might have caused violence. He needed to find out information about Stan. Without family or even close friends to draw on, he needed to find someone who knew him. He called Roger Walsh, the golf course superintendent, and asked, "Who were Stan Fedewa's friends at your course?"

"He's a loner, keeps to himself."

"Did he have a drinking buddy, a mistress, a neighbor, someone in an organization like AA, or maybe a church?"

"Yeah, a church. He was active in a church out of town, a Pentecostal church, I think. I don't know the name of it, but a checkbook or email list should give you that name."

Lou called Detective Wheeler and asked if Stan had any correspondence referencing a church. Russ answered quickly. "There were some checks written to the Church of God in Wyandotte."

"Thanks, Detective. Has your staff talked to anyone at this church yet?"

"No, we have not."

"I'll let you know what I learn."

Lou called the Wyandotte church and was put through to the pastor, Wayne Hillbreth. "Pastor Wayne, this is Lou Searing. I'm a detective working on the murder of Stan Fedewa."

"That's sad; we've lost a good man."

"I'm sure you did. Are you planning a funeral?"

"No, his wish was for no attention to himself. He wanted to be cremated, with no service, so we'll do what he asks."

"Did you know him?"

"You could say that. We shared a cold beer on occasion, and we hunted together—deer season mainly."

"My guess is you know him quite well then. Hunting and beer-drinking buddies usually know a lot about one another."

"What do you want to know?" Wayne asked.

"Did he have any skeletons in his closet?"

"Plenty of them."

"Give me one or two, please."

"He was a reformed drug dealer. At one time he was a well-connected dealer of heroin in this county. He took in a lot of cash, and he was lucky that the authorities never arrested him. He found Jesus on a hunting trip while I was with him. He realized that drugs were ruining lives and families. So, on a dime, he went clean. One minute he was a drug kingpin, and the next he was free of the business. Not only that, but he dedicated his life to rehabilitating people who wanted to get clean."

"Becky?"

"Yes, Becky is a good example."

"Do you know where she is?" Lou asked.

"No, she is very unpredictable. She will be gone for days at a time, and nobody knows where she goes."

"Back to skeletons, please," Lou said. "Any others in the closet?"

"He was a scam artist, preyed on older adults, usually women. He conned them out of their money."

"Whoa, I thought he was this reformed criminal, and you say he cons older people?" Lou asked, surprised.

"The word I have is that he wasn't as active as he once was, but he still couldn't seem to help himself when he saw a sitting duck."

"This guy was some catch," Lou said, shaking his head. "Disturbing fellow vendors at craft shows is nothing compared to conning seniors and selling drugs."

"Well, he was a charmer. He made a good first impression, and then people fell for his schemes. At the craft shows, he undercut competition and upset fellow vendors. At the course he didn't keep the fairways cut to perfection or get morning dew off the greens in a timely manner."

"I hesitate to ask, but are there any more skeletons?"

"Those are the only two I know about. He did give generously to the church and I enjoyed his company, but I seemed to sit on his good side. I pity anyone he didn't like. He could make life difficult if he didn't like you."

"Well, somebody caught up with him. It's my job to find out who that was."

✂

Lou was exhausted as he pulled into the Searing driveway south of Grand Haven. Lou greeted Carol with a hug and a kiss. He brought his suitcase into the house, then checked back mail. He asked Carol if there was anything he needed to know, but she had nothing for him.

Once unpacked, with dirty laundry put in the hamper, Lou was ready for a stroll along the shore. The Searing estate, as most referred to it, was perched on a dune on the Lake Michigan shore. Lou and Carol loved to take evening walks along the lake's shore, walking hand in hand, discussing this and that, and just enjoying being together.

Carol picked up a couple of Lou's favorite chocolate chip cookies in a napkin and put them in a tote bag. Leaving Sami and Sami II at home, the two set off for their favorite pastime.

"What's this case about, Lou?" Carol asked, always curious about Lou's investigations.

"Looks like a classic case of someone having a reason to take a life, so he or she did. The victim was quite a character."

"How so?"

"Stan was an ex-drug kingpin, con artist, disrespecting of colleagues."

"Did he have any redeeming qualities?" Carol asked.

"He's a church member, interested in reforming drug addicts. His pastor liked him; he was Stan's drinking and hunting buddy."

"How was he killed?"

"It appears to be a stabbing. We think it was a surprise attack from behind."

"Where did the murder take place?"

"In the vendor's tent."

"Seems like an odd place for a murder. The killer is taking a chance of being detected," Carol observed.

"Taking a chance puts it mildly. The possibility to be seen or heard was high. But, no one has come forward to report anything."

"Could the killer be one of your vendor friends?" Carol asked.

"Could be, but I doubt it. We are always ticked off about this and that. We're human. But, in the fifteen years I've been selling books at craft shows, I've yet to meet anyone with a mean streak."

The two sat on a huge piece of driftwood, quietly enjoying being together in a relaxing moment. Carol produced the cookies. Each had one, smiling with each bite.

After fifteen minutes in this paradise, Lou said, "Guess we had better get back. It'll cool down soon."

The two stood, took each other's hand and proceeded south along the shore to the Searing home.

"I got so interested in your case, I forgot to ask how sales went in

Houghton Lake," Carol remarked.

"It was a good show. I think I sold about 140 books. I ate at Shaker's in Prudenville. They sell my books, too, as you know. I can't thank those folks enough."

"They're on display at the checkout counter as I recall."

"Yes. A good mystery and some mints—an interesting combination."

"And, Kathy in Arnie's Crafts sells your books as well?" Carol asked.

"Yes, Kathy sells many. She's a valued customer."

"You are blessed to have these people willing to sell your books to their customers."

"Indeed."

The next day Lou asked Detective Wheeler if he might see the autopsy report but it hadn't been completed yet. "Have you found Becky?" Lou asked. "Did anyone call with information?"

Russ had nothing to report.

"He did say, however, the *Detroit Free Press* is taking a strong interest in this case, Lou."

"Why is that?"

"It happens, usually because the victim is well-known among subscribers."

"Stan can't be a local icon," Lou said.

"Who knows why an editor features a story?" Russ began. "Maybe it's murder in Farmington Hills. Maybe it happened at a public event, like a craft show. Your guess is as good as mine."

"Are they doing investigative reporting or covering your work?" Lou asked.

"They have a phone line where people can call in tips. They've assigned a reporter to the story, and not just a beat reporter."

"So, you have a major newspaper, me, you, and your fine staff."

"Lots of company for this one," Russ said.

"If this reporter calls, do I talk to him?" Lou asked. "By the way, what's his name?"

"Not a 'him', Lou. Her name is Marcia Abbott, and she's good. I can't fault her at all. Her standards are high, she's responsible and professional. The only difference is she has the resources of a newspaper and her contacts to help her. All we want is to solve the case, and who gets the credit is not our concern."

"Hmm, Marcia Abbott. Don't know why I haven't heard of her."

"She is relatively new to Detroit. She was in Phoenix before moving here. She has solved three or four cases since her arrival. If it makes you feel good, she has heard of you, but then you're a recognized name, certainly, among private investigators."

Chapter FIVE

L ou got a call from the women's shelter. "Mr. Searing?"

"Yes."

"This is Heather, the receptionist at the Abused Women Shelter. Detective Russ asked me to inform you that Rebecca Dawson has been found. She has contacted us to say she has moved. She asked that her personal items be shipped to a forwarding address."

"Where is that?" Lou asked.

"I knew you were going to ask that, but I don't know."

"I asked an intern to do the job, so she did. I gave her the note with the address. She said she threw it away and has no paperwork from the post office."

"Do you remember where it was to be sent?"

"I think I saw 'Missouri', but it could have been 'Mississippi'. I am sure it started with the letter 'M'."

"Thanks. What was in her belongings?"

"Clothes and toiletries is all. She didn't have a lot, and when she was gone for days at a time, she never took much. She sort of lived with the clothes on her back."

"Do you know why she moved, and why she wouldn't stop back at your shelter to pick up personal items?"

"She had no car, so she took a train or a bus. I'm not sure of that because she probably couldn't afford public transportation. Someone probably drove her away."

"And you wouldn't know who that would be?"

"No, there was some guy in her life. But we don't ask, and she didn't offer, so we don't know who he was."

✂

Lou called Jerry. "Becky is gone, apparently out of state."

"I still think she is involved in some way," Jerry responded.

"I agree. I have no other news, but I just wanted you to know about Becky. I need to talk to Mike from Mackinac Island Fudge. He's a good thinker."

Within the hour, Mike returned Lou's call.

"Thanks for being available. I've learned that Becky Dawson, the woman who worked with Stan in his booth, has left the state."

"They're a couple of screwballs," Mike offered. "I'm not surprised. Listen, I believe in Karma. If you don't, that's fine with me, but if you con enough people, if you mess with people's lives and businesses, it's going to come back at you. Murder is a bit of a stretch, but it all comes back. Good begets good, and evil begets evil in whatever form it is expressed."

"I agree, Mike. I respect your thinking. Do you have any ideas?"

"Thanks for your confidence in me. I think something will pop soon. Just be patient. Listen to me—advising you, a successful detective."

"I appreciate your words, Mike. Thanks. I wish I had a piece of your sugar-free chocolate fudge. I think it might tease my investigating skills to jog a bit."

"The next show we share, I'll see that you and a large chunk of our fudge get together."

"Okay! No reason to keep you from your day's work, but if anything comes to mind, please give me a holler."

✂

Lou called Cory thinking that time often opens the memory box and provides something forgotten about earlier. Lou asked Cory to recall the day of the murder. "What's on your mind?"

"Stan Fedewa was a real pain in the ass. As soon as I saw him at the Farmington Hills show, I knew I would lose it. And, sure enough, I did."

"What angered you?"

"I'm sure you've heard the rules: no undercutting, no advertising outside of the booth, and so forth."

"So when you say you would lose it, I assumed you confronted him."

"I did and I talked to the show director, and fellow crafters. I was quite angry."

"Did you talk to the woman working in his booth?"

"Yes, I even bent her ear."

"What did she say?" Lou asked.

"She said he was acting inappropriately. She was embarrassed."

"So, she was sympathetic to your concerns?"

"Definitely."

"Did she offer to talk to him or act on your behalf?"

"No, she just listened. She understood my frustration and then turned to help a customer."

"Did she say or do anything out of the ordinary?"

"I don't recall. It was an ordinary interaction. Now that you have mentioned it, I remember asking her if Stan had a tax license to sell in Michigan. She said she didn't know, but doubted it. She said Stan wouldn't have anything to do with government. I continued to question her. I said, 'I'll assume there's no license here. Is that a fair statement?'"

"'Works for me,'" Becky replied.

Lou followed up with the Michigan Department of Licensing and Regulation.

"Licensing office, Lucy speaking."

"I'm calling to report a violation of Michigan law," Lou began.

"What is your name please?"

"Lou Searing."

"Who do you suspect of violating the law?"

"His name was Stan Fedewa."

"And, the violation?"

"I can't cite a law, but he's selling at a craft show and has no sales tax license."

"I'll check his name. What is the name of his company?"

"Pens and More."

"Ok, I'll pull it up on my computer. One minute, please."

"Thank you."

"You appear to be right. I haven't a record of his name or the name of his company. I suspect if he doesn't have a sales tax license, I doubt he's paying tax on his sales."

"I'd be surprised if he did."

"I'll file this complaint and get back to you with action we take. Give me your contact information - email or phone number."

Lou complied with her request. "One more question, please."

"Sure."

"Does it matter that he's dead?"

"Dead?"

"Murdered, actually."

"Well, there is no action we can take. If I were you, I'd let it go."

"Can't you put a lien on his properties?" Lou asked. "That way his executor would have to pay the State for Stan's offences."

"I don't think so, but I'll ask our attorney."

"Can you please let me know what you find?" Lou asked.

"I'll make a note to do so."

"Thanks."

"Oh, where was this guy murdered?"

"Farmington Hills, Michigan."

"Oh, was that the craft show murder?"

"That's the one."

Chapter SIX

The case lay dormant for a couple of weeks as no leads surfaced. This was on its way to being Lou's first unsolved murder. Lou monitored his smartphone for email messages or phone calls. He checked in with Detective Wheeler every few days and each time he was promised he would be contacted if and when Russ learned anything.

Lou received a call from a vendor who was unknown to him. "Lou, I'm Georgia Myers. I want to talk to you about the craft show murder. I'm relatively new to the craft show world, usually at the end of a line of booths. I make and sell embroidered towels and blankets. I have some thoughts that may be helpful."

"I'm more than willing to meet you. Where do you suggest?" Lou asked.

"I live in Holland."

"Holland is down the road a few miles."

"Could we meet at your home?" Georgia asked.

"Definitely. When?"

"Anytime."

"I'm home now; if this is good for you, drive up. Do you know where we live?"

"I do. We often drive on Lake Shore Drive, and I have seen your sign by the road. So, I know where you live."

"Okay, come on up. We may not have any chocolate chip cookies but I'll have hot coffee or iced tea, if you'd like some."

"Thanks. Coffee sounds good. I'll be there in an hour."

✂

When Georgia arrived in her Porsche, Lou went out to greet her. "Wow, the craft business must treat you well to have you driving around in luxury."

"Believe me, craft show income contributes nothing to this car. My husband is a successful stock broker, and with the economy doing well, we are not hurting."

"Come on in. I'm anxious to hear what you have to share."

"I hope Carol is home. I want to meet her. I feel close to her when I read your books. She sounds like a beautiful person."

"Thank you. Yes, she is that for sure. And, yes, she's home."

Lou introduced Georgia to Carol, who gave her a short tour of the Searing home.

"Your home is just as you describe it in your books. I can see why you enjoy living here."

"Let's just say it is our 'Porsche'." The two chuckled while Carol was without a reaction. She decided not to ask for clarification. She'd have it explained during the evening walk along the shore.

"Would you like some coffee or tea?" Carol asked.

"Coffee would be nice."

Carol approached the two. "Here is your coffee."

"Thank you very much."

Lou took his notebook off the counter as he was anxious to get down to business. "Would you like to sit on our porch?"

"That would be nice, but could we talk down by the shore?"

"Sure."

The two walked a few hundred feet to the shore.

Lou began. "You wanted to talk to me. I'm anxious to learn what you have to share."

"I trust you, Lou, and I think you can help."

"I'll do whatever I can."

"Well, I can't believe I'm about to say this, but I helped kill that craft guy." Georgia, with head down began to sob, her tears falling onto the sand.

"You killed him?" Lou couldn't believe what he had heard.

"Indirectly, I did. Maybe I was an accomplice to the murder. I didn't pull the trigger, but I was a party to his death."

"Why confess to me and not to the police?" Lou said.

"I talked to my minister who told me to talk to you and to take your advice."

"I guess I appreciate the referral, but authorities really need to know about this."

"No, no, please don't push. Listen to what I have to say."

"Okay. Go on."

"If I say anything, I have been threatened with my life and I know if word gets out that I ratted on the killer, I'm dead. And, quite frankly, I don't want to go there."

"What did your minister think I could do for you?"

"He simply suggested I talk to Lou Searing. I trust him, and here I am."

Lou put his arm around Georgia's shoulder, and said softly, "You need a hug." The two embraced as Georgia continued to sob. Lou and Georgia sat down in two beach chairs nearby, and after some moments of silence, Lou began.

"When you're comfortable, tell me everything you came here to share."

Georgia, holding Lou's handkerchief, took a deep breath, and seemed composed.

"I can't believe I've confessed," Georgia began. "I've just pulled an imaginary trigger. I should have just kept quiet."

"Needless to say, I'm surprised," Lou replied.

"That vendor was evil. I know you'll think I'm sick, and maybe I am. But as sad as I am because I cooperated in taking a life, I know that I rid the world of this poor excuse for a human being. After the guy was killed, I returned home and have kept to myself since."

"How did you know that I was on the case?" Lou asked.

"On your website was an item explaining that you were currently investigating a murder, one at a craft show in Farmington Hills."

"So, I take it you told no one about this except me." Georgia nodded.

"Did Mr. Fedewa harm you in any way? What happened that caused you to support another in killing him?"

"He ripped off customers. One of my regulars came to my booth and asked, 'Do you know what that vendor selling pens is telling people? Your crafts are from China—you didn't make them. He said you got them for pennies, while you give people the impression that you made them.' I couldn't believe what I was hearing. My heart began beating rapidly. I almost blacked out and was filled with anger. I knew at that moment that I would want him dead."

"Premeditated?"

"Definitely. I discovered a like-minded person who felt stronger than I about ridding the earth of this tyrant. We plotted his death. The killer went to The Knife Man's booth and purchased a knife. I had some wire in my tool box at my booth. The plan was to entice him back to his booth after dark. The killer told him he wanted to discuss a money-making plan. Stan invited the killer into his booth. The fact that it was raining a bit helped him to invite me into the booth, also. The killer

57

suggested Stan sit down as a folder was placed in front of him. The killer said, 'Take a moment to look this over and then we can talk.' Stan opened the folder and before he had looked at the first page, the killer brought the knife up and around him while plunging it in and out several times. To be sure of the kill, the killer wrapped the wire around his neck and pulled it tight for several seconds. We stepped out of the booth, pulled the zippers down, and walked away, feeling sure nobody had seen or heard anything. In fact the two of us were surprised at how little effort was involved. With the outpouring of revenge we felt at peace. I sensed hundreds of people applauding, thanking us for ridding them of this devil."

"I am pleased, if that's the right word, that you sought me out and told me of this experience. But, I must ask why you're telling me?"

"I wanted to confess, and you are the only one I trust."

"Now, we're both between a rock and a hard place," Lou explained.

"How so?"

"You admitted to being an accomplice to a murder but don't want your confession known, for the killer would kill you for telling of the murder. I'm with you between the rock and the hard place because I now know about the murder of Stan but if I report what you told me, the killer might kill you. So, we both have a secret to keep."

"Yes, we're partners in this cramped space," Georgia nodded solemnly.

"Let me think on this. I won't go to the police right now."

"Thank you, Mr. Searing. Thank you for your mercy."

"Now that you have my support I'm going to ask you to continue trusting me and tell me some more about this murder. You said the murder was committed by one person and that you were in on the planning of the crime."

"Yes."

"You keep referring to the murderer as the killer. Is that a man or woman?"

"A woman."

"A crafter?" Lou asked.

"I'm not going there. I'll give you just enough information to solve it, but I won't squeal on my partner."

Lou and Georgia went back to the house. Lou opened his notebook and wrote down what he had just heard. Seeking the last page, he passed a notation that a customer of Cory's said she was angered that Stan was bothering her friend Cory, and that she had told Cory that she just may need to step up and take some action. Lou thought, *Could this woman, unknown to Cory, be the murderer?*

"We know how to contact each other," Lou told Georgia. "No one needs to know we met, and we can't meet again. On my website (www.buttonwoodpress.com) is an opportunity for subscribers to follow activities of Buttonwood Press. I suggest you go to my website and become a subscriber. When I send messages I can send words that will only have meaning to you. If a response is required, snail-mail me your response. This will allow us to communicate without fear of messages being intercepted."

"I need to notify the authorities, but I won't do that until we are assured this partner of yours is locked up or dead."

"Thank you, Lou. My minister was right. You were the one to advise how to seek justice avoiding my life being threatened."

"I'm not an attorney. You'll need one, a very good one. Does your husband know any of this?"

"No, oh no, this would bring down his empire. I'm pretty sure there's a mistress. So, he would not have my back. If this ever comes out, I won't be in a Porsche any longer."

"Also, you need a counselor that you trust," Lou advised.

"I don't know who to go to," Georgia said plaintively.

"I'll recommend someone."

"I'm sorry to put all of this on you, Lou."

"Happy to help you."

"So, I just go home and live as usual for the next few weeks?" Georgia asked.

"Yes. In the meantime, I have work to do. I will contact you with the names of a lawyer and a counselor. Thanks for coming forward."

"Thank you, Lou, for not judging me, and for getting me some help."

"You're welcome. By the way, if something breaks before I get back to you, do not offer any information."

"Something breaks?" Georgia asked, appearing confused.

"The police could knock on your door, you could get a suspicious phone call—anything out of the ordinary."

"Can I go out, or should I just stay home?"

"You can go out. Live as you've been living."

"Thanks, and please thank Carol. She is a beautiful person."

"I will."

On her way home Georgia realized that she should not have confided in Lou. Whatever happened in the future was nothing but a sad outcome for her and her husband. The cat was out of the bag, and as nice as Lou was, the confession was loaded with nothing but negativity: arrest, court, years in prison, and years without drugs, to say nothing of her Porsche.

Chapter SEVEN

That evening during their walk along the shore, Lou presented his dilemma to Carol. "Something happened today that hasn't happened before."

"Does it involve your visitor today?" Carol reasoned.

"Yes. She admitted involvement in the killing of the vendor. It appears to be rage, revenge, and possibly the expression of some personality defects."

"So, you drove her to the police station?" Carol asked.

"No. She explained that her talking to me might be a death sentence if the killer learned she had squealed. So we're both between a rock and a hard place. I also promised to get her help with a lawyer and a counselor."

"That's nice. You can't assume she's not guilty because she admitted assisting with the killing. Tell me again how you know her."

"She's a vendor I've seen at a number of craft shows. I don't know her well, but she is a gifted embroiderer who lives in Holland. Now that I think about it, her booth was across from mine at the Coast Guard Festival craft show in Grand Haven last year. She's a nice lady, quiet, not one to talk much to other vendors."

"I don't understand your dilemma," Carol said.

"For some reason I didn't, as you say, 'drive her to the police station'. I have standards as a detective and yet I felt some compassion for her. I wanted to take time to formulate a course of action."

"That doesn't sound like you, Lou. You would show compassion, but the Lou I know would take her to the police. After all, you know her to be guilty. If a person admitted guilt to a police officer, that officer would immediately put on the cuffs and take her in."

"Yes, but I'm not a police officer. If someone admitted killing someone to a priest or lawyer, neither may feel compelled to drive her to the police station."

"You are not a priest or lawyer," Carol reminded Lou. "But, I respect you, and I'll support whatever you think best."

"I'll record, in as much detail as possible, my discussion with her this afternoon in case I've put myself in jeopardy by not turning her in."

"I enjoy talking about your cases, Lou. Thanks for sharing."

"You're always helpful, Carol. Let's head back to the house. I could use a cup of hot chocolate before watching some television."

✄

The next day, Lou called Jack Kelly in Muskegon. Jack is Lou's go-to-man when it comes to researching people and advising on a number of issues. Jack is approaching sixty years of age, handsome, has a full head of hair and a well-trimmed goatee. His mother, Elaine, lives with him.

"Good morning, Jack." Lou opened.

"Yes, it is a good morning. What's on your mind?"

"I've a new case."

"The craft-show murder, right?"

"Right."

"As soon as the news report came on television I knew you'd be on this one. It's right up your alley. Did you know the victim?"

"I've done a couple of shows with him, but never had reason to talk with him."

"I read in the *Detroit Free Press* that the guy's name was Stan Fedewa. I was so sure you would investigate this murder that I got to work before you asked for help."

"You're kidding," Lou replied.

"Not kidding. I just figured from past investigations that you're going to want to know everything you can about certain people. The victim was undoubtedly one, so I got to work."

"And…"

"The victim's full name is Stanley W. Fedewa. He was sixty-one years old. His home was in Troy. He's got a police record. There have been several arrests but not much punishment. There always seemed to be some reason to not give him jail time or a stiff fine. He made his money by gambling, believe it or not. His game of choice is Texas Hold'em poker. He was addicted to these games and on most nights he walked out of the hall with five to six hundred dollars. He had no family. Never was married. He worked for a golf course in Oakland County. Perhaps you know all of this, Lou?"

"Some of it I know, but you're giving me good information."

"You know about the crafts. He bought pens from a distributor. He pays next to nothing for them. He then claimed he made them and sold them for around fifty bucks each. He drove a fancy car, was almost always smoking a cigar. If he absolutely must not smoke in a particular place, he'd chew on one. He had a real oral fixation problem if you ask me. He spent his winters in Gulf Shores, Alabama. He was a different guy down there—no big car or fancy clothes. He resembled a homeless man, staying in shelters and gambling to make ends meet."

"So, in a sense he lived two lives," Lou concluded. "I may have to go down there to see what else I can learn about him and his mode of operation. Thanks, Jack. Great work. There's another person I need you to research. Her name is Georgia Myers. She lives in Holland, Michigan. She is a vendor of detailed embroidery. She called me and visited the same day. Please work your magic and tell me what you can find out about her."

"I'm on it, Lou. Is she a suspect?"

"She's more than a suspect, Jack. She claims to be an accomplice."

"Okay, I'll call once I know something."

✂

Lou called Detective Wheeler in Farmington Hills. "I have a lead on the craft show murders."

"Excellent work, did you get your man? How do you solve these things so quickly?" Russ asked.

"Whoa, not solved. I said I had a lead."

"What is it?" Detective Wheeler asked.

"I need your support on this. I have an informant but if it gets out that this person came to me, we'll likely have another murder on our hands. Please let me work with the information I have, okay?"

"Sure, do what you need to do. If you're close to solving it or when you get close to solving it, don't embarrass me by letting me go down a rat-hole."

"I wouldn't do that, Russ."

"While you're on the line, I've something for you."

"Any information is good," Lou responded. "What do you have?"

"Marcia Abbott, the *Free Press* investigative reporter, called to say they got a tip."

"And, what was that?"

"The killer is thought to be a woman who is not a crafter. She is quite tall. That's it. No name or physical description other than being tall."

"Does the *Free Press* tip-line allow for a follow-up contact?"

"Yes, if we think the information is useful, we can contact the tipster."

"Are you going to contact him or her?" Lou asked.

"Yes, I'll follow up on this tip, and we'll keep each other in the loop."

"Sounds like a plan," Lou replied.

Russ called the tipster, who had been at the Farmington Hills craft show and witnessed the drama between Stan and Cory. She said a tall woman was carefully watching the interaction and also taking pictures of the victim's booth. The tipster admitted that's all she saw and had no credible reason to think this tall woman killed the vendor but she said the woman was suspicious and not acting normal.

Russ thanked the woman and called Lou to share what he had heard.

"Thanks," Lou replied. "You never know what people see and how they feel about it."

Russ said he would contact the show surveillance video people and see if the woman can be spotted.

"Thanks. Let me know what you find."

✂

Lou called Jack. "Just checking to see if you found anything about Georgia Myers?"

"I was going to call. I don't have much. Her past and present are night and day."

"How's that?"

"I found what you told me, but I went further. Are you sitting down?"

"No, but whatever you say won't faze me."

"Georgia Myers is as you noted: wife of a wealthy stockbroker who lives in Holland. Her hobby is embroidering. But, dig into her past, and you'll see a woman you wouldn't want your son to take a liking to."

"Explain."

"The best words to describe her are, 'reformed drug addict'. Her past shows she had a serious drug problem. She's been in and out of rehab, has a police record, and on and on. It's a sad story. She was a socialite in Grosse Pointe who got caught up with the wrong crowd. Her parents admitted her to a rehab facility in California that caters to the wealthy. She was admitted and released a total of four times."

"I assume she got clean."

"Yes, and this is where your visitor comes full circle. Somehow she connected with Stan Fedewa who apparently was rescuing addicts."

"How did she end up with a wealthy stockbroker?"

"Steven Myers met Georgia at the California rehab facility. They had a tryst, and a baby. They married, moved to Michigan, and started over, so to speak. He has stayed clean and remains successful in his community."

"Great work, Jack! I've a call on my cell and I need to take it. I'll be back to you soon."

✂

Lou looked at his caller ID and saw that his neighbor, Brad Nix, was calling.

"Lou, you know I'm not particularly nosy, but that Porsche in your driveway yesterday sure has the neighbors curious. Are you buying that car from someone?"

"No, you're not nosy; well, yes you are, but it's a good kind of nosy. I want my neighbors to be observant."

"Phil, on the other side of you, told the rumor mill that the vehicle has an Ohio license plate."

"I took a photo of the Porsche and if you ever need a photo of the owner, I have it in my cell phone."

"You might have gone a bit too far, Brad. Noticing a license plate and a sticker are one thing, but taking photos of my guest is a bit much."

"For all I knew, you were talking with a suspect in one of your cases, and might just need a photo of your visitor."

"Actually, I do need a photo of this woman. Can you send it to me?"

"Sure. "

"Thanks, Brad."

"Can you share information? The neighbors are wondering who your guest was."

"Just tell everyone who asks that the woman was helping me with a case."

"Will do. Sorry if I overstepped my bounds. I was just trying to be helpful."

"You were, and I'm thankful, believe me."

✂

Lou turned his attention to Becky Dawson. He requested a copy of any police reports, including Stan's autopsy report. Because of Russ's support of Lou's request, the Oakland County sheriff acquiesced and forwarded the requested information post haste.

After reading the reports, Lou was convinced beyond a reasonable doubt that Becky probably killed Fedewa, or at least was involved in the killing.

Becky's sister had contacted Detective Wheeler by phone.

"I'm Darlene Dawson, Becky's older sister. Our mother asked me to call and tell you what you need to know."

"Thank you. We couldn't easily find family members so I'm glad you called."

"What can I help you with?" Darlene asked.

"Our main question would be, do you know if Becky killed Mr. Fedewa and then skipped town?" Russ asked.

"To be honest, she hung out with some real low-lifes," Darlene admitted. "But to answer your question, no, we don't know who killed that man."

"Did Becky have unsavory friends or acquaintances?"

"She was married once but the honeymoon, if there was one, only lasted a couple of weeks. Her husband abused her pretty badly and she had the good sense to get away from the jerk."

"What was his name?"

"We only met him at the wedding. Becky didn't talk about him much. They were married by a judge at the county courthouse so I was able to get a copy of the marriage license. The husband was listed as Rod Hastings, and his address was the Salvation Army shelter. Becky supplied this guy with drugs. I suspect that's why he abused her, because she couldn't always get drugs and the guy went nuts."

"She worked at a golf course. Correct?" Russ asked, even though he knew the answer.

"I guess so. She went from one part-time job to another. I didn't hear about a golf course, but she certainly could have worked at one."

"She also worked for a vendor who sold pens at craft shows?" Russ asked hoping for additional information.

"Actually she admitted to me once that she hated the guy and she stole money from him. He didn't do a good job of accounting for sales. She knew it was wrong, but she figured he didn't need the money. He didn't seem to want for money. He had a Cadillac—doesn't that give you some idea of income, by hook or crook?"

"Do you have anything else to share?" asked Detective Wheeler.

"Again, we just want to help. If you need pictures, samples of handwriting, names of people, we'll help."

Russ took Darlene's contact information. "We'll want to talk with you further. Also, a private detective, Lou Searing, is working on the case and he will want to interview you. I'll pass along what you have shared to Mr. Searing."

"Is that the guy who solves crimes and then writes a book about each case?"

"Yes, that's him."

"Becky has all of his books. She likes his writing style."

"If you think of anything else that will help us find your sister, please call me at the number you dialed to reach me. Again, I am Detective Russ Wheeler."

Chapter EIGHT

Russ called Lou to inform him of the developments. "This case is a series of crazy twists and turns."

"How's that?"

"I just talked to Becky's sister."

"I didn't think she had family."

"The sister, Darlene, said she called at the urging of their mother."

"What did you learn?" Lou asked.

"She said Becky has read every one of your books."

"Thanks, I guess."

"She said that Becky thought of Stan as a monster and she stole from him, figuring a man with a Cadillac wouldn't miss the money."

"Anything else?"

"She was married for two weeks to a guy whose address was the Salvation Army shelter. She supplied him with drugs and to show his appreciation, he abused her."

"May I talk to, or visit, Darlene?" Lou asked.

"Yes. I told her about you and that you would want to talk with her."

"Thanks for this call, Russ. I'll see what I can find out."

Talking with Darlene was top priority. Arrangements were made to interview her the next day at her home in Dowagiac.

When Lou was greeted by Darlene, she was unkempt, looking like she had just woke up which might have been the case.

"Thanks for meeting with me," Lou said.

"It was Mom's doing. The last thing I need is to star on 'Dateline NBC'. I don't miss my sister. We're as different as night and day. But, Mom felt we should help the police."

"We can use anything you can share." Lou looked at what appeared to be a family portrait on the living room wall. "Is Becky in this photo?"

"Yes, on the far left of the second row. I am on the opposite side."

"May I have a copy of this photo?"

"Not a problem. We have a couple of 5 x 7s. I'll get you one. And, I'll put the names on the back so you will know who is who."

"Thank you."

"Oh, I'm sorry. I didn't offer you any coffee. As I recall from your books, you like your coffee black, with chocolate chip cookies. I'll see if I can find some in the kitchen."

"I'd love it. Thanks."

While Darlene was in the kitchen, Lou viewed framed photos scattered through the living and dining rooms. Under the family photographs, Lou noted a short stack of mail. He quickly scanned the envelopes. He saw a letter addressed to Rebecca Dawson. He took out his cell phone and took a photo of the address.

As Darlene reentered the living room with refreshments, Lou spoke up. "Who's this in the photo in the dining room?"

"Oh, actually that's about the only one we have of Becky smiling. Do you recognize the men in the photo with her?"

"No."

"I'm surprised. The two men are the FBI detectives who solved the Unabomber case. Becky is fascinated by people who solve crimes. She's intrigued by their reasoning skills. Some people collect photos of movie stars or athletes, but Becky enjoys meeting and talking with detectives. This explains why she's a fan of yours, and why she enjoys your books."

"Do you know the names of any of Becky's friends?" Lou asked.

"Can't help you there."

"Did Becky belong to a church?"

"You've got to be kidding. Her shadow doesn't cross a church of any denomination."

"Her residence?" Lou continued his questions.

"Salvation Army shelter, jail, homeless shelter, abused women shelter—pick one."

"I guess this is it for now," Lou said, handing Darlene his card.

RICHARD L. BALDWIN

"Please contact me if anything else pops into your head you think I should know."

"I will. Would it be too much to ask you for an autograph of your latest book?"

"I don't have copies with me, but I will see that you get a copy."

"Thank you, Mr. Searing."

On the way to Grand Haven, Lou received a call on his cell phone. He pulled off the road to answer it.

"Lou? Jack here. I've got something you might find helpful."

"Glad you called, Jack, as I have information for you, too. You go first."

"The woman who visited with you, Georgia Myers, has been found dead. Police are calling it a suicide. She left her car running in a closed garage and died of carbon monoxide poisoning."

"Where was that?"

"At her home in Holland. There was no note. Her husband is devastated. Police quoted him as saying she seemed depressed for the past few days."

"This case is driving me crazy," Lou said, sounding quite dejected. "Let's meet face-to-face, verify what we know, and decide what we need to do from this point on."

"Name the place and time, and I'll be there."

"How about Panera's in Grand Haven tomorrow morning?" Lou suggested.

Jack said, "Would ten o'clock be okay?"

"Great. Thanks."

"You can tell me your news tomorrow or if you want me to know now, go ahead with your news."

"It can wait till tomorrow," Lou stated.

"Fine, see you tomorrow morning."

✂

Lou and Carol were walking along the shore behind their home.

"You look perplexed, Lou," Carol remarked.

"That's probably because I am."

"What's got you in its grip?" Carol asked.

"It isn't easy to explain."

"Try and maybe in saying what you're thinking it will help clarify the confusion."

"Good idea."

Hand-in-hand with ripples of water moving over their feet and ankles, Lou began.

"I have two dead people. One is Stan Fedewa and the other is Georgia Myers. They are both craft show vendors."

"Good, that much is clear and known."

"Stan was murdered in his booth. Georgia committed suicide."

"At first I thought Becky killed Stan and I still have that as a possibility."

"As to Georgia, she recently appeared at our door and claimed to be involved in the murder. She was driving a Porsche and told me she was married to a wealthy stockbroker in Holland. Then I get connected with a woman named Darlene who is Becky's sister."

"So, who is the woman who visited you, and why does she confess to killing Stan?"

"She was Georgia Myers; she is now dead, as I said, suicide."

"So, two dead—Stan and Georgia," Carol repeated. "And, Georgia told you she was an accomplice in Stan's murder and could be killed if talking to you was learned."

Lou nodded. "I can't rush to a conclusion here, but it could be a murder-suicide, as simple as that."

"This has been one of our longer walks," Carol admitted.

"My favorite time of the day, being with you, walking along the shore, and except for my ramblings it has been peaceful."

The coming weekend was a craft show for which Jerry and Lou had both registered. They would have an opportunity to connect and examine each other's brains for a clue or theory. The show was set-up was in the Northview Community Center. It was a first-class show with high-end crafts. And, would be the first time that Cory would be free of Stan and his inappropriate behavior.

After the men had set up their booths, they sought their complimentary coffee and donut. They sat at a table in the cafeteria, hoping others chose not to join them.

Jerry remarked, "Got yourself a tiger by the tail with this one, huh?"

"No case is a piece of cake, but this one is a challenge," Lou admitted.

"You'll solve this one, too. You always do."

"I appreciate your confidence, but the day will come when I can't claim that. It could be this time, but I expect to solve it."

Their privacy was interrupted when a fellow crafter approached.

"Well, if it isn't two of my favorite crafters, taking a break before the show opens."

"Hi, Toby," Jerry replied. "I didn't think you were doing this show."

Toby turned to Lou. "I hear you're working with the Farmington Hills Police, trying to solve Stan's murder."

"I can't seem to pass up a challenge," Lou admitted.

"Well, I didn't expect to see you here. I have a tip for you. It'll either open a door or give you indigestion." Toby grinned.

"What do you have, Toby?" Lou asked.

"When you get a break, stop by Chelsea's booth. She sells yard signs. And her booth is by the front door."

"I know of her, kind of tall, ponytail, keeps to herself."

"That's her, Chelsea Porenta. If you can figure out what fashionable pens have to do with yard signs, tell me, okay?"

"Tell me more," Lou offered.

"I could be wrong, but she's selling pens that look like pens Stan sold at past shows. If I'm right, you explain it," Toby said. "You're the detective, not me."

"Was she at the Farmington Hills show?" Lou asked.

"Don't know—I wasn't there. But, since I alerted you to this side bar, keep me posted on what you learn. Fair?"

"Oh, sure. Stay tuned."

Toby left Jerry and Lou to finish their coffee and donuts. The show was about to start. "Let's go to Chelsea's booth and see these pens. And, if she is alone, how about you lure her out in the hall and give me time to nose around the booth a little." Jerry nodded in agreement.

The two men approached the booth to find front and center, a display of pens. Jerry got Chelsea's attention. "Would you please join me in the hall for a minute or two? I'd like to ask you something in private."

Chelsea answered. "I don't see anyone approaching so I can chat for a moment." She and Jerry left the booth and headed for the hallway. Glancing left and right, Lou immediately entered the booth and looked under the display tables. A mailing label on a large box caught his eye. The box had been shipped to Stan, and it contained several boxes of pens. Lou had what he needed and inconspicuously left the booth.

On their way to their booths, Jerry asked, "Find anything?"

"Under her table was a box of pens from China, and the label was addressed to Stan."

"Interesting."

"Two things enter my mind," Lou said.

Jerry answered quickly, "She killed Stan or she stole the pens."

"Or, she innocently bought them from Stan before he was killed."

"Are you going to ask her about how she came by the pens?" Jerry asked.

"Yes. Do you want to listen ?" Lou asked.

"I'd rather you go alone and tell me what she says."

"Fine with me."

A bit later, Lou asked his booth neighbor to watch his booth while he was gone for a few minutes. He walked to Chelsea's booth; the timing was perfect because she didn't have a customer at that moment.

"These pens look like those Stan Fedewa sold before he was murdered," Lou began.

"That's because he gave me a box of them. He said I'd done him a favor and he wanted to repay me."

"Excuse me for being nosy, but what was the favor you did for him?"

"You know, I don't know. It sounds odd, but I can't imagine what I did. He may have thought I was someone else, but I thanked him. Then he died, and so I'll never get clarification of the favor I did. Since he gave me the pens, I figured I could sell them."

"That's a nice windfall. No upfront costs and every pen you sell is clear profit."

"My lucky day and I'm long overdue."

"When did he give you the pens?"

"The first day of the Farmington Hills show.

"And, you said he gave you a box. Does that mean a small box, or a large shipping box?"

"Small box."

"I see. I assume you know he was murdered that night."

"Yes, common knowledge."

"When you heard that he had died, you didn't inform the police about this gift?"

"I never considered it. I didn't do anything wrong. He came up to my booth, handed me the box, and left shortly thereafter."

"I need to get back to my booth," Lou replied. "Thanks for talking with me."

Stan's murder was the main topic of conversation among vendors at the Northview show. People were understandably nervous, since nothing even close to a murder had ever happened at a craft show. Most of the comments were of the variety of "He had this coming to him," or, "This is his Karma. He was a menace and it all came back to him." No one had any idea who killed him. Each figured it was probably due to some activity outside of the craft world.

Lou was unwilling to accept Chelsea's explanation of how she came upon the pens. It was a gut thing. He had no reason to suspect Chelsea was a thief or murderer, but her explanation was too simple. Lou couldn't see Stan giving merchandise to anyone, let alone a fellow vendor. Either Stan didn't want to divulge the real favor, or there was no favor to start with. But, Lou thought, *This doesn't make sense!*

Around noon, visitors to the craft show were startled when a fire alarm went off. There was a mad rush for the front doors. The director of the show quickly got on the loud speaker. "There is no fire, repeat, there is no fire. A child accidently tripped the alarm. You do not need to leave. We'll explain what happened. We apologize for this startling event. Please return to your shopping. Again, we apologize for this disruption."

The vendors were very nervous that something had happened that was criminal. Blood pressures rose and heartbeats quickened, but once their host assured everyone that the alarm was explainable, heartbeats returned to normal.

Detective Wheeler felt he could relax a bit. With Lou on the craft show murder, more pressing crimes demanded his attention. As he studied a pattern of home invasions, a man walked into the police station asking for an opportunity to talk with him.

"What is it you want to talk to Detective Wheeler about?" the receptionist asked.

"The craft show murder," the man replied.

Russ was taking a phone call, so he told the receptionist he would be out to greet the guest. The call took longer than expected, and when Russ walked into the reception area, no one was there. He asked the receptionist, "Where is the person who wanted to talk to me?"

"I guess he got tired of waiting and left."

"Did he sign in or mention who he was?"

"I didn't ask for a name. Do you want to check the security video?"

"Yes, please make sure the video is not erased."

When Russ viewed the security tape, he didn't recognize the man and his car had not been positioned for a view of the license plate. Nor could the make of the vehicle be ascertained. It was an SUV, and for the most part, SUVs all look alike.

"If he comes back, contact me immediately and assure him I will make myself available on the spot."

"Will do, Detective."

Lou called Russ. "Would you, at your convenience, send me the list of what was in Stan's booth when the forensic team filed their report?"

"I'll fax it to you momentarily. While you're on the line, a guy came to our station and asked to see me about the craft show murder. He got impatient having to wait and left. I have our security video tape and will be studying it soon."

"Thanks," Lou replied. "If a guy shows up wanting to discuss the murder, I'll be sure to respond and will send you what I learned."

"Thanks. Make sure your fax machine is working because I'm going to send the list you wish."

Lou called his neighbor, Brad Nix. "I'm calling you in an official capacity. You are my eyes when I'm not home. There's a man who might pull into our driveway wishing to talk to me. If a vehicle comes into the drive and neither Carol nor I are home, please discreetly note the vehicle make and model and license plate, state and number. If you are comfortable, you can approach the him and ask if you can help him. Let me know what you learn."

"Will do, Lou. When do I get my badge and my gun?" Brad said with a laugh.

"There will be no ceremony to make you a deputy."

"That's probably good because my deputy fee is probably beyond your ability to pay."

"And, let me make this clear. I don't want you greeting every occupant of a car entering our driveway. I don't need nor want Barney Fife with his single bullet in his shirt pocket."

"I understand. But, could I be invited to your beach party next summer?"

"That's fair compensation."

Lou had not heard from Jack in a few days which wasn't like him. He usually responded within a day to Lou's requests for information. Exactly at the moment he was thinking about Jack, he pulled into Lou's driveway. He knocked on the front door.

Lou opened the door and let him in.

"What do I owe my pleasure of your company?" Lou said.

"I decided to visit you in person," Jack said looking concerned. "For the first time since we've worked together, I've been threatened."

"Come on in. In what way were you threatened?"

"I got a phone call from a woman who said she knew where I lived.

She advised me to stop feeding you with information. She said I ran the risk of ending up like the murdered craft show vendor. She ended the conversation with, 'Just know that I will always know where you are and what you are doing'."

"I'm so sorry, Jack. Until this gets solved, I will not involve you. You and our friendship are much too important to play games with some psycho."

"Thanks, Lou. Like you, I don't scare easily, but at the same time, I don't want to foolishly put myself in harm's way."

"Absolutely not. Just lie low, and don't call me, email me. We can't play a card without knowing who's threatening us."

"I think that's best."

Lou suggested, "You might consider going on another mission trip with members of your church."

"That's an idea. I'll call our pastor and see when the next mission trip is scheduled."

"Whatever you do, don't challenge the threat. Go along with it till we know about it."

"Thanks for understanding, Lou."

Jack's receiving a threat was disconcerting to Lou. The last thing he wanted was for something to happen to Jack because of his friendship and his skill in helping solve a crime.

Lou and Carol were eating dinner when their phone rang. Usually during sharing a meal, Lou and Carol won't answer unless they know who is calling. Lou got up from the table and looked at caller ID.

"It's Elaine Kelly. I've got to take it," Lou said as he picked up the phone and heard, "Lou, Jack hasn't come home. About four hours ago he said he was going to meet with you. He always tells me where he's going and when I can expect him home. This isn't like him. I don't know if he was in an accident or if he needed to be taken to a hospital."

"I'm sorry Elaine. I'll do what I can to contact him. I assume when you call his cell, he doesn't answer. And, I assume when you send him a text message, he doesn't respond."

"That's right."

"He left here about three hours ago," Lou recalled glancing at his watch. "He didn't say where he was going, but I assumed he was going home. Have you called the hospital or the State Police?"

"No. I'm very worried. Something is wrong because this is not Jack."

"Stay by the phone," Lou advised. "I will make some calls and try to find him."

"Thanks, Lou."

"Sure. Would you like Carol to come up and stay with you?"

"You're most kind, Lou. If she's available, I'd appreciate it. I'm not only worried about Jack, but maybe I'm in danger, too."

"Carol will be up as soon as possible. In the meantime, don't answer the phone unless you know who's calling. Don't open your door to anyone. Also, write down everything that has happened and continue to keep a diary. Detail everything."

"Thanks again, Lou. I'll wait for Carol."

There was no question that Carol would go to be with Elaine. As Carol was backing out of the garage, Lou said, "Have you got your phone?"

"In my purse. Love you."

Lou placed a call to the Grand Haven State Police post. "State Police. How may I direct your call?"

"I would like to speak with Commander Robertson. Please tell him Lou Searing needs his counsel."

"Please hold, Mr. Searing."

About twenty seconds later, Lou heard Robertson's voice. "How can I help you, Lou?"

"I'm calling to request you direct your troopers to be on the lookout for my assistant, Jack Kelly. He was seen in Grand Haven about four hours ago, and heading home to Muskegon. He should have been home a few hours ago. His mother is quite distraught. He always lets Elaine know his whereabouts and plans. I know a certain amount of time must elapse before declaring someone missing, but I'm asking you to see this as critical and act immediately."

"We will, Lou. Describe the vehicle."

"He drives a blue late model Ford Escape. He has a vanity plate. The letters are IMALSA."

"I'll put the word out and I assume I'll make you the contact if we find him."

"Do I need to call hospitals or police officials?"

"No, we'll handle this."

"Thanks, Commander."

Carol called Lou after settling in at the Kelly home. "Elaine is almost a basket case. I hope she can relax a bit. She's hyperventilating. She asked me to call her doctor. The doctor will be arriving soon."

"Anything else?"

"No, I've got the TV on and also called her best friend to pay us a visit."

"Obviously, Elaine cannot stay alone overnight. Either she comes home with you or you plan to stay overnight. If you want me to join you, just say so."

"Let's see what happens. He could be found any minute and we can begin to relax."

"The Commander at the State Police post is calling. I've got to go. Thanks for your update."

"Yes, Commander. What do you have for me?" Lou asked.

"I'd like to tell you we found him, but we haven't. I need to talk to Mrs. Kelly, or I need to ask you for some information."

"I think you should talk to Elaine. I'll call her and explain that you need to talk to her. Carol is there offering support. Give me your number and she'll call."

Commander Robertson gave Lou the number to call.

Lou relayed the number to Carol and asked her to encourage Elaine to call the Commander. "Tell her there is no bad news. He just needs some information to help his staff find Jack."

Within a half-hour Elaine had a support crew at her side: her best friend, her doctor, Carol, and a couple of neighbors.

Elaine was quick to call Commander Robertson.

"Lou asked me to call you."

"Yes, Mrs. Kelly. I need to ask some questions."

"I'll do my best."

"Does Jack take any medications?"

"Yes. He has his little pharmacy, as we like to call it."

"I'll need a list, please. Has he had any fainting spells?"

"No, that has not happened."

"Has he had episodes of not knowing where he was?"

"No. Jack is very independent."

"Has he fallen asleep while driving?"

"Not that I know of."

"Ok, thank you. I've notified hospitals, state police, county sheriffs, and local police departments to search for your son. We are doing all we can."

"I appreciate it, sir."

Chapter NINE

That evening, when Lou had the chance to open his mail, he found a handwritten letter from Sylvia Chappen. Curiously, he read it on the spot.

"Mr. Searing, I'm a freshman at Grand Haven High School. One of my classes is titled, 'Finding your Vocation'. We have to interview someone who has a job we would like to consider for a career. When I grow up, I want to be just like you. May I interview you, or even better, could I work with you in solving a case? My email is detectivetobe87@coldmail.com. If you would like to talk to my parents or teacher, let me know. I hope to visit with you. Thank you. Yours truly, Sylvia Chappen."

Lou responded quickly by email. "Please set up a time when you, your parents, and I can talk."

✄

Carol called Lou. "The police do not want Elaine to leave home, so coming home with me is not an option. I'm not terribly comfortable staying here, but I'll do it. The police will monitor the house all night, so we are safe, but I would rather be doing a crossword puzzle or watching 'The Voice'."

"You are so kind. I'm proud of you."

"Be sure and let me or us know whatever you learn."

"I will. Love you."

"Love you, too."

Nothing happened during the nighttime hours. Neither Jack nor his vehicle was located. Elaine's doctor had given her medication to calm her nerves. No one called or visited except relatives and friends. It was as if time stood still. Constant worry dominated the minds of all concerned.

Lou was aware that in some situations, a car can leave the pavement, and go down a ravine and not be seen by passersby. The driver is sometimes unable to exit the car. A cell phone may not be within reach or not even with the victim.

Lou was a friend of Tom Howard, a pilot who flies out of the Grand Haven airport. Lou called Tom and asked if he would take him up and fly over a few possible routes that Jack could take in driving from Lou's home to his home in Muskegon.

Tom was home and as usual would do whatever Lou needed to solve the mystery. It was ten a.m. when Lou arrived at the airport. Tom was ready to go. Lou boarded the plane that was near the airport office and waited for Tom to complete a last-minute flight inspection.

Lou briefed Tom on Jack's disappearance and Lou's theory that he might have gone off the road. He could be stranded and out of sight of any walkers or drivers. He much appreciated Tom giving him an aerial view. Lou was torn: he didn't want to find a crashed car, but he did want to find Jack.

The Cessna took off, lifted, and banked to the right. For a moment Lou forgot the purpose of the mission, taken in by the beautiful shoreline of Lake Michigan and the Tri-cities: Grand Haven, Spring Lake, and Ferrysburg. He snapped back to reality when Tom asked, "Which way do you want to try first?"

"Let's follow a direct route up US-31 to Jack's home." The route was flanked with businesses. There was little vacant land, and the land was flat so there was no ravine to drive into.

As the plane came over Tucker Avenue, southeast of Muskegon, Tom said, "Okay, give me another route or an area you wish to view from above."

"Let's go south following Harvey Ave. On occasion, Jack takes this way home."

Tom banked south between Harvey and Quarterline Road where the land was less populated. Again, they saw nothing, but Lou's gut told him to turn and cover the same area, so Tom did as Lou asked. About three miles south and east, Lou saw a bright flash lasting for no more than a second. The sun was reflecting off of something shiny on the ground. Lou was curious, so he asked Tom to turn and head south.

Once again he saw the flash of light but that was all.

"Can you contact the police from up here, Tom?"

"Yes."

"Okay, please call State Police Commander Robertson in Grand Haven."

Tom turned to a frequency that would let him communicate with someone on land.

Lou asked Tom, "How do you describe the place where we saw the flash of light?"

"I'll talk to the police after you make the connection," Tom replied.

Within a couple of minutes, Lou was talking with Commander Robertson explaining what he was doing and what he had seen. Tom heard over the drone of the engine, "Tom Howard, my pilot, can explain the approximate location for your officers to search." Lou handed the microphone to Tom.

"We saw a flash of light northwest of Fruitport on Sheridan Road, just south of Mount Garfield Road."

"Understood."

Commander Robertson sought a helicopter to search the area, while Tom and Lou returned to Grand Haven airport. After thanking Tom, Lou called Carol. "Tom took me up in his plane. We saw a couple of unexplainable flashes of light just west of Fruitport."

"It could have been a signal from Jack," Carol said.

"Yes, or it may just be a reflection off some shiny object. The State Police will search the area in hopes of locating the source of the flashes."

"What should I tell Elaine?" Carol asked.

"I wouldn't say anything to get her hopes up, but some news keeps hope alive. I trust you'll do what you think best for Elaine."

✂

The helicopter hovered over the area of light flashes, flying closer to the earth than a Cessna could. "Look there," said the pilot, pointing to the left of the chopper.

"That looks like the car we're looking for." The copilot called the Commander to report a vehicle similar to the Kelly car had been spotted.

The Commander ordered a ground unit to check the area of the car sighting for there was no possible landing area for the helicopter within a mile or so of the vehicle. As Lou suspected, Jack's car was down in a ravine, out of sight.

✂

The ambulance pulled up to the Hackley Hospital in Muskegon. The trauma team removed the unconscious body of Jack Kelly. A medical team did quick assessments en route to a bay in the emergency room.

The head of the trauma team said to others around the gurney, "He is alive. Go ahead with the examination. We'll assess next steps once we know the state of his health." Turning to the nurse he added, "Let his family know he is alive and encourage them to get here as soon as possible."

✂

The nurse believed Commander Robertson to be the one who would know how best to contact the family. She called the Commander and told him of the doctor's request. Once Lou heard from Commander Robertson, he called Carol and gave her the news. Lou also suggested that Elaine's pastor join them. "Jack's alive, but I'm still waiting for a description of his injuries."

Carol said, "Should the family get to the hospital soon because Jack is close to death or to give Jack support?"

"I can't help with that one. I was not told he was near death. I'll cautiously say the doctor wanted love around his patient."

"I'll tell Elaine the news and drive her to the hospital. Are you going to the hospital, too?"

"Yes."

"See you soon."

Carol joined Elaine in the kitchen where she was sitting at the table having some tea. "I was talking to Lou," Carol began. "He said that authorities have found Jack. Apparently he went off the road and down a ravine. He's alive but that's all I know about his condition. The attending physician wants you to go to the hospital as soon as possible."

"Thank God. Thank you, Jesus," Elaine said, giving her Lord credit for Jack's being found and alive.

"Lou suggested that your pastor may wish to be with us."

"I'll call him and ask," Elaine said. She followed by asking, "Do you think the hospital has alerted our doctor?"

"I have no idea," Carol said. "It might be a good idea to call and alert him or her."

"Thank you. Our doctor is Madeline Zuckerman. If she's available, I know she'll stop whatever she's doing and go to Jack's side, too."

Within a half-hour Pastor Hillbreth, Dr. Zuckerman, Lou, Carol, and Elaine were in a conference room waiting for Dr. Harvey Westbrook, the lead doctor on the trauma team. The door opened and Dr. Westbrook entered to find Jack's family and friends. Ten eyes were fixed on the doctor.

"Thanks for coming. I have been monitoring Jack since he was admitted around 10:00 this morning. He was unconscious upon arrival and remains so. Soon I would like you, Mrs. Kelly, Pastor, and Mr. Searing to enter his room. Talk to him as you normally would. Don't assume he can't hear you. His vitals remain satisfactory."

"How will he look?" Lou voiced what everyone was thinking.

"If you are wondering if there are visual injuries you can expect to see, the answer is no. Surprisingly, he will appear as he would if he were home in bed. He has some IVs so we can feed him. He will also have an oxygen tube with airlets in his nostrils. He does have a head wound but that is bandaged."

"Is he going to live?" Elaine asked, bracing herself for what she might hear.

"The next day or two are critical. We hope and trust he will awaken from the coma. Then we can better predict his prognosis. The fact that his vitals are normal offers hope that Jack will recover after therapy and rehab."

"Can we see him now?" Elaine asked.

"Yes."

Investigating the murder of Stan Fedewa took a back seat while attention was given to Jack Kelly. Now, a high priority was to find Becky Dawson and Lou was thinking of driving to Delaware, Ohio.

Lou called Detective Wheeler to find out if he had tried to reach him with news.

"We've had a serious accident near Muskegon," Lou began.

"Who's involved?"

"My right-hand man, Jack Kelly, was found in his car at the bottom of a ravine in rural Muskegon. He's in the hospital in critical condition. There may be some crimes committed, but I can't be sure of that now. He's in a coma."

"Sorry, Lou. I know he's a good friend and a key player on your team."

"Thanks. I expect a full recovery. At least I'll put a positive face on it. But, the reason I'm calling is to ask if there have been any developments in our craft show murder?"

"It's been quiet. I haven't prioritized the case, figuring we had deputized you, and if it can be solved, you'll do it."

"Does that mean I'm on the payroll?" Lou asked with a chuckle.

"If you'll take Monopoly money, of course! And you might get a raise any day now."

Both men chuckled. "I will get back to the case while keeping attention to Jack's needs."

"Okay, please call me with any news about Jack."

"Will do."

✂

Elaine led the entourage into Jack's private room. Maintaining her composure she approached Jack, took his hand, and kissed him on the forehead. "Jack, honey, Mom's here. You'll be up and around soon. If you can hear me, please squeeze my hand." There was no squeeze.

Pastor Wayne Hillbreth took Jack's other hand and then said, "Let us pray. Oh Lord, we are hopeful for our son and friend, Jack. Guide your servants, the doctors and nurses at this hospital. Hold your servant Jack in your heart. In the name of your son, Jesus Christ our Lord, we pray."

Lou moved to Elaine's side, touched his friend's arm. "Hey, Jack. You've got a lot of people praying for you. I can't wait to be working with you real soon. This case and others can't be solved without your help. If you know this is Lou Searing, blink."

Elaine was sure she saw some movement but admitted it could be a twitch. She leaned down and kissed Jack again. "You rest, son. All will be well. I love you."

The three left the room and returned to the reception room.

Once again Doctor Westbrook entered the room. "How did Jack look to you?"

"I'm so thankful he's alive," Elaine answered. "I pray he'll wake soon. What happens now?"

"We'll monitor Jack and supply him with nutrients, oxygen, and medications to lessen pain. Elaine, I would like you to spend as much time in the room with him as you can, talking to him, holding his hand. You should talk frequently about memories of things he enjoyed. Do you and Jack have a dog or cat who could visit him?"

"No, we don't."

"Does he like dogs?"

"Yes."

"Does he have any allergies to dogs?" Dr. Westbrook asked.

"None that I know about."

"If it's agreeable, I will ask a volunteer to bring in a therapy dog. It's amazing what the smell, sounds, and feeling of the pup pressing on him can do."

"That's fine. When will Jack come out of his coma?"

"I wish I could tell you. All we can do is comfort him and wait for him to awaken. That could be shortly, or days, or weeks could pass before he regains consciousness. The important thing is to give him stimulation. Read the Bible to him, play music, and talk to him as you would at the dinner table. Approximate reality whenever possible."

"Shall I go home at night?" Elaine asked.

"We can bring a rollaway bed so you can sleep in the room if you'd like. Food is in the cafeteria. Your choice. Keeping you feeling comfortable is important. You're a most important member of Jack's medical team. Others can give you a break, perhaps church members."

"Thank you. I would appreciate a rollaway bed in Jack's room. Thank you for your kindness."

✂

Lou and Carol went home, fed Sami and Sami II, checked mail and phone messages. It was getting late, but Lou and Carol didn't want the day to pass without their walk on the shore, its being the height of the summer with daylight peaking about 10 o'clock. They walked to the shore with a bright moon casting its reflected light on earth.

"Quite a day," Carol said with a sigh.

"Yes, for sure."

"What do you think happened to Jack?"

"I've a hunch, but will await the police report."

"Tell me your hunch."

"It's pure conjecture on my part. I have no basis for what I'm about to say, but…"

"Go ahead."

"For one thing, the car went into the ravine as it was coming south," Lou recalled. "Why would he be driving south? He must have gone home and found Elaine gone and so he drove south?"

"What caused him to go off the road?" Carol asked.

"Your guess is as good as mine. I'm thinking it was some malfunction—failed breaks, tire explosion."

"Let me be a devil's advocate and suggest his car was tampered with," Carol offered.

"Or he swerved to avoid an oncoming car," Lou suggested.

"Or he panicked at the sight of a deer or other animal running across the road. What about his injury?" Carol asked.

"If he had an airbag and a seatbelt on, I can't imagine sustaining an injury that would cause him to lose consciousness. I'll wait to see photos of the car where it came to rest."

Carol asked, "Did he hit a tree, or a boulder?" She quickly followed with, "The conversation is interesting but there will be no answers until we see the car and read the accident report."

"You're right. Guess I need to turn my attention back to the craft show murder. I will move forward thinking Jack's accident was not related to the murder."

With attention on Jack, Lou forgot about Sylvia who had wanted to interview him. He checked his email and saw a message from her. A meeting was scheduled for the day after tomorrow. Lou thought, *What experience could this kid have that would offer a bit of drama yet be assured no harm would be forthcoming?*

In advance of the meeting Lou called Mrs. Chappen. "This is Lou Searing. We have a meeting in a day or two to discuss how I might help Sylvia with a school project."

"Yes we do and thank you so much for your willingness to help my angel. I'm so glad you called because a briefing would be good for you and Sylvia."

"Good. Tell me what's on your mind," Lou offered.

"Sylvia is different."

"Every teenager is different, right?" Lou asked with a grin.

"Yes, but Sylvia is a rare teen. There is not a label that fits her. For example, she dresses in whatever character is on her mind."

"Okay. Do kids make fun of her all the time?" Lou asked.

"No, thankfully. She has gone to Grand Haven schools since kindergarten. The kids grew up accepting the personality quirk. They know she's not a threat. She is exceptionally popular. She was voted to the junior high homecoming court. Yes, she dressed as Cinderella for the dance."

"Am I to think how this fits into the interview?" Lou wondered aloud.

"She will appear as Sherlock Holmes or Colombo, or Jessica from the show 'Murder She Wrote'. She's not trying to be funny or to be disrespectful to you. It's just who she is."

"That's not a problem. Anything else?"

"When dressed in character, she often plays the role."

"For example?"

"If she appears as Colombo, she very well could wear a trench coat, have a dog with her and God forbid, have a used cigar between her fingers."

"Okay, thanks for telling me. I can handle this. Anything else?"

"She's highly intelligent, has excellent manners, quite beautiful if I say so myself."

"If it is appropriate, is it agreeable that she ride along with me as I investigate?"

"We trust you completely, so yes."

"Is she mature enough not to role-play the fantasy in reality? By that I mean, she would not do or say something inappropriate?"

"You will find her an interesting person and she is quite mature for her age. Well, I say that even though she occasionally becomes a little kid wearing a holster and cowboy hat."

"I will not put her in harm's way and you'll always know our travel plans. I'll always be clear about what I suggest she do. Do you understand?"

"Absolutely."

"I may even ask you to go along on an occasion or two."

"Not a problem."

"Now this work is not like a TV show," Lou reminded Mrs. Chappen. "This isn't entertainment where a case is solved in an hour. In fact, there's no glamour involved, to say nothing of an occasional difficult situation."

"I think she understands this."

"Okay, I'll see you and perhaps Colombo, soon."

"Thank you, Mr. Searing."

Chapter TEN

Lou was awakened early next morning by a phone call from Detective Wheeler.

"Lou, sorry to wake you so early this morning."

"Not a problem. I work 24/7 when investigating."

"I figured and that's why I called."

"What can I do for you?"

"I got a call from a sheriff in Ohio. They have a murder at a craft show in Elyria. Do you want to join me in a trip to Elyria to see if there are similarities?"

"For sure. But, in this day and age, can't information be shared with Face-Time or Skype?"

"Yes, but I want to be on-site. It will be a day trip. Is your day open today?"

"Yes."

"I'd like you to join me as soon as you can get here."

"I can be on the road soon. Wait. How about I ask my friend Tom Howard to fly us there?"

"I'll drive and you fly," Russ replied. "I'll have authorities pick you up in Elyria."

"Assuming Tom is available. Can Tom be reimbursed by Farmington Hills for this trip?"

"Yes."

"Thanks. See you in Elyria, and I'll stay in touch with you by cell. Before you go, can you tell me about the murder to satisfy my curiosity?"

"There are some similarities. Murder at night in a booth. Weapon was a knife, but in this case, a lot of valuable items were stolen."

"That's enough. I'll be in touch, Detective Wheeler."

Lou called Tom who said he could fly him to Ohio, but he'd have to get excused from a meeting at the Chamber of Commerce related to the Coast Guard Festival.

"Thanks, Tom. I'll assume you will be excused, so I'll meet you at the airport."

As Lou was about to leave home, he heard his fax machine beckon him. He went to his second floor office and took the fax papers, fastened them with a stapler, and put them in his valise. Carol was not up yet, so he left a note explaining his plan for the day and undoubtedly into the evening. He ended with, "Looking forward to another late evening walk. Love you. Lou."

At the airport, waiting for Tom to arrive and put his Cessna through the mandatory preflight procedures, Lou took the faxed material from his valise and began to read.

The medical and the police accident reports from Jack's mishaps were now in Lou's hands. *This is going to be interesting reading. I hope some clues appear,* he thought.

He looked through the accident scene report. The vehicle appeared to hit a tree head on. Lou thought, *If Jack lives, he will be one lucky man.* There was no evidence of an animal involvement. The brakes were not faulty. Blood on the dash board and front window explained Jack's head wound. Jack had not been wearing a seat belt and the air bag had not been deployed. It appeared the vehicle left the road at a higher-than-posted speed.

Next, Lou read the medical report. After wading through a lot of medical terms, he concluded that Jack had suffered a collapsed lung, significant head trauma, and damage to both knees.

Lou reread both reports, this time keying in on the investigating officer's report. The car was going south on Sheridan Road northwest to Fruitport. *Jack shouldn't have been going south—not if he was returning home after talking to me,* Lou thought.

Lou heard the approaching Cessna. He returned the papers to his valise, left the office, and after the propeller stopped whirling, he stepped up and into the plane sitting beside Tom.

"Welcome, Lou," Tom said. "We've got a great day for a long flight."

"Great and thanks so much for helping me out. The City

of Farmington Hills will reimburse you for your service. I appreciate you, friend."

"Let's get this bird up and off to Ohio," Tom replied.

The Grand Haven airport was without a control tower. Tom spoke into his handheld microphone to alert pilots in the area of his intent to fly southeast.

After enjoying the take-off and scenery, Lou settled in for the four-hour flight. He checked frequently for any text messages.

One was from Carol: "Jack is showing some signs of coming out of the coma. The therapy dog seemed to do the trick. If our dog licked my face repeatedly, I would come out of a coma as well. Love you."

Lou responded, "Great news. You said 'showing some signs,' what do you mean?"

Carol responded almost immediately. "Blinking, squeezing a hand when asked to do so."

"Thanks. Keep me posted."

Between Lou's hearing loss and the engine noise there was little communication with Tom. Lou loved flying. Because of his familiarity with Michigan, he could easily spot cities, highways, and landmarks.

Tom contacted the airport in Elyria, seeking permission to land. It was given. Tom brought the plane to earth as if a feather were floating to the ground. He had also asked for the police department, requesting a pick-up for Lou Searing. So, by the time Tom had taxied to the designated tie-down area, a police vehicle had arrived.

"I think I'll go into Cleveland and visit the Rock and Roll Museum," said Tom, announcing his plans for the day. "Call me on my phone about an hour before you will be ready to return to Michigan."

"Okay. How will you get to downtown Cleveland?"

"I'll rent a car."

Lou went to the awaiting Elyria police car, and Tom went into the airport office to get a car for his drive into Cleveland.

At the Elyria Police Station, Lou was greeted by the police chief and Russ.

"Welcome to Ohio, Lou." Russ said, extending his hand for a handshake.

"Flying sure beats driving," Lou said with a smile.

"Let's go into the conference room," Russ suggested. "We can discuss the case and then we'll go to lunch on our way to the scene of the murder."

"Sounds like a plan," Lou replied.

"Our host has a carafe of coffee and I ordered out for chocolate chip cookies," Russ explained. "You are living the life of a king, Lou. A free flight from and to Grand Haven, coffee and cookies to stimulate your brain."

"I thank you. I just hope your expense and my work day ends up worth your inviting me here."

"I want us on the same page. With that, let's get to the murder. On the table are reports of the murder, the autopsy, crime scene photographs, and witness comments. I can leave you and allow you time to go over all of it, or I can go over this with you."

"I go for the latter," Lou advised. "Two heads are always better than one."

"Ok, I'll be back in a minute," Russ said, standing and leaving the room. Within a minute Russ returned with another officer.

"Lou, this is Sergeant Jake Huckabee. Sergeant, this is a private detective, Lou Searing. He's working on the case with our department."

"Nice to meet you. Are you the detective mystery-writer?"

"Yes."

"I've read some of your books and I've enjoyed them. Your main character lives in a fantasy world. The real world is quite a bit different from his world."

"Oh, I realize that. All of my stories are fiction so I have the liberty to tell my story without violating anyone's trust."

"Who is Richard L. Baldwin?" Jake asked.

"I let the writer in me, fictitiously named Richard L. Baldwin, write the story of my investigations."

"Each book is a good read," Jake said with a smile. "Thanks for great storytelling."

"You're welcome. The pleasure is indeed mine."

Russ spoke. "I've invited Jake to join us while we review this material. I want him to share anything that could help us see a pattern here."

"I'll be in and out as I have responsibilities to deal with today," Jake said.

"We understand. We appreciate whatever time you can spare," Lou said.

Jake got Lou's attention and began. "Okay, let me give you basics—the victim was a woman who sold her jewelry at craft shows. It appears she was lured into her booth sometime between the end of the show on day one and the next morning when the show opened for day two. The cause of death was stabbing. There were no witnesses. It appears the killer made off with hundreds of dollars worth of jewelry. Other vendors said there was an ugly exchange between the show's manager and the victim, but the manager had a viable alibi and is not a suspect at this time."

The three discussed ideas, reviewed reports, and viewed photos.

"I will admit that we may have a copy cat crime," Lou said, feeling quite sure this wasn't a chance killing. "I think if we solve one of the murders, we'll likely have solved two murders."

"I couldn't agree more," Russ said.

Lou continued, "I don't know if you're aware, but these days the vendors are not just local folks offering crocheted washcloths. These do exist, but the vendors of today come from all over and the extent this is true correlates with the popularity of the show. So, the killer could be someone who lives in a distant state and is making the circuit of summer shows."

"Thanks, Lou."

Lou looked at Jake. "I know we'll visit the park where the show was held, but, is the park secured? It's obviously an outdoor show. Did the show hire security? Is there video anywhere in the park? Do vendors who travel from show to show in their campers, camp in the park?"

Jake looked up from his notes. "Yes, the park is secured. The entire area is fenced. There are three gates and from 10:00 p.m. to 5:00 a.m. the gates are locked."

"So, if someone is camping, they are locked into the park during the seven hours," Russ summarized.

Lou interjected, "Is there a number to call if a camper needs to get out?"

"Yes, that's presented in their packets at check-in."

"On the night of the murder, did any camper call to solicit someone to unlock the gate?"

"To be honest, we didn't look into that."

"Do you have a list of all vendors and where they're from?"

"We don't have that, either." Jake admitted.

"You'll want that list," Lou suggested. "Also, if the show manager asked for license plate numbers on the application, I'd like to see them as well."

"I should have answers to both your questions before you leave today."

"Thank you, but there may be more than these two," Lou replied. "Continue, please."

"Yes, it's an outdoor show. There was no security inside the park. The police drove by several times during the hours the show was closed. There are no video cameras inside the park."

"Thank you."

The three men reviewed reports and chatted for approximately three hours. Lou and Russ decided to go to lunch and continue the conversation. Officer Huckabee arranged to meet them at the park where the show was held.

During lunch, Russ and Lou discussed what they had learned. Russ remarked, "You've given me a whole new way to look at the Farmington Hills Craft Show murder."

"How's that?" Lou asked.

"I'm leaning toward a vendor killing a fellow vendor. Remember the vendor now selling pens that belonged to Stan?"

"Yes. That's not normal, whether Stan gave her the pens or not," Lou remarked. "I've been selling my books for more than a decade and I've never seen another vendor sell items another vendor gave him or her."

"We need to note everything that the vendor sells in his booth. I'll tell you this, if crafts belonging to the victim are for sale in another's booth, you can get out the cuffs."

Lou added, "If you can somehow match a suspect's camper in Elyria to a camper in Farmington Hills, a search may very well turn up goods stolen from each murdered vendor."

"Thanks, we'll work on that angle."

Russ paid the bill and the two began driving toward the park, the scene of the murder.

On arrival, they saw Jake standing outside of his squad car. Russ drove to the vehicle and parked.

"So, lead us to where the booth was when the vendor was killed," Russ directed Jake.

The three men walked about fifty yards. "Here it is," Jake said. "If this tree could talk, we have our murder solved and from what you've said, your crime might be solved as well."

"As expected, there's nothing to observe except the layout," Russ said.

"I've got some questions," Lou said.

"Take a stab at it, pun intended," Jake replied.

"This road in front and behind the victim's booth is gravel?"

"Yes."

"Did the victim have a mat or rug on the ground inside the booth?"

"I'll have to ask our forensic staff that question."

"Sometimes vendors have a rug, or interlocked foam mats that you see in preschools."

"I'll have that for you when we return to the office."

"What happened to everything in the booth where the murder took place?" Russ asked.

"Other than evidence, it was all picked up by the victim's daughter."

"We'd like her name and contact information, please," Lou said.

"Sure."

"I'll tell where I'm going with this," Lou said. "If there was a rug, mat, or foam flooring, I'd like your staff to pick up the covering and put it with evidence. I will want to know if any footprints are visible, or even a part of a footprint."

"We will have that for you," Jake said, noting the request on his notepad.

"Thanks. Now I'd like to see where the campers park during the show."

"That would be in the back of the park, over there," Jake said pointing toward the camper section. "Do you need to go there?"

"No, just curious where a camper might be in relation to the victim's booth. I'm not suggesting that the killer had a camper, but it's a viable scenario."

Satisfied that he had done all he could in Elyria, Lou looked to his host and said, "Well, Jake, I guess unless Russ needs me for something else, I'll fly back to Michigan."

"We appreciate you and Russ coming here. You've given us plenty to look into. We'll be in touch."

"Here is my card if you need to contact me, but it's probably best to go through Russ."

"Will do."

Russ offered, "I'll take Lou to the airport and then I'll stop at your station for a few minutes before heading home. You promised some information. I'll forward it to Lou."

Lou called Tom and said he would be ready to go in an hour, but for Tom to take his time.

While he waited, Lou checked his email. All that was worth noting was an email from Sylvia confirming their meeting in the morning. Carol texted that Elaine is feeling calmer and seems more accepting of her reality. Jack is improving, but the doc said he will have a rough row to hoe before he gets back to normal, if that's possible.

Lou sent Carol a text saying the day had been a good one. It looked like there was a connection between the two craft-show murders. He hoped to be home early enough for a walk along the shore.

Tom's Cessna touched down in Grand Haven at 8:10 p.m. Lou arrived home at 8:45, and he and Carol were on the beach five minutes later. "The walk feels good," Lou remarked. "I've been sitting most of the day and most importantly, I'm with you. Best part of the day!"

"Tell me about your day," Carol said.

"First, is there news about Jack since you sent your text mid-afternoon?"

"No news is good news. Elaine said she would call when there is anything to say."

"Ok. Thanks for supporting her. You continue to be a walking saint."

"Okay, right. Now, tell me about your day."

"Not much to tell. Smooth flight to Elyria. Met with police about their craft show murder. After lunch Russ and I surveyed the park where the murder took place. Then it was another smooth flight home. Tom is not only a good friend but an excellent pilot."

"Are you closer to solving your case?" Carol asked.

"Only in that I have more information than I had early this morning. There is no suspect that's clearly on the radar. Every case has that screw-up that often leads to the case being solved."

"That reminds me; I ordered a T-shirt for your birthday."

"A little early, isn't it?"

"Yes, but I couldn't resist this one."

"Do I have to wait till October?"

"No, you'll have it in a day or two."

"Cut the suspense. Tell me, please."

"It is a T-shirt that reads, 'Bad Choices Make Good Stories'."

"That's my business!" Lou exclaimed! "Thanks, it's a perfect gift."

"Glad you'll like it. Shall we sit on our driftwood or head home?"

"I vote for going home."

"That would be my vote as well," Carol replied. Hand in hand, the two headed home as the sun touched the horizon near Wisconsin.

Chapter ELEVEN

L ou pulled up to a McDonald's in Holland on time to meet his 9th grade protégée. He immediately spotted Sylvia, thanks to her mother's description of who he might see at this meeting. Sylvia was wearing a trench coat, held a stuffed toy basset hound, and woe a wide-brimmed hat. Lou walked up and said, "Sylvia, I presume."

"Yes, Mr. Searing. It's an honor to meet you. I think you're the first author I've ever met."

"The pleasure is mine."

"This is my mom, Harriet. I am a minor, can't drive, and I'm always in need of an escort."

"I understand. Hello, Mrs. Chappen."

"Hello. Thanks for meeting with us."

"Sylvia talked with me on the phone so I have a pretty good idea of what she is looking for."

"Yes, why don't you tell Mr. Searing what your project requires?"

"I am to write a report about working with someone whose job is what I would like for a career."

"May I attend when you give your report?" Lou asked, genuinely interested in Sylvia's perspective.

"You would really do that? Wow, is that cool or what?"

"Would you like to interview me or just go along on an investigation?"

"Both, please."

"Then I'll make one request of you," Lou said.

"What's that?"

"When you're with me, please dress 'normally' and I'll tell you why. You can't stand out in any obvious way—you need to be inconspicuous. I want you to be a typical 'kid'. I don't want any clothes or actions that would draw attention to you. I want you to watch, or trail, or whatever I will ask you to do. Understand?"

"Yes. I won't wear clothes that draw attention to myself."

"Whatever you wear is totally up to you and fine except when you are part of my investigations. If you can't do that, I can't take you along to experience being a detective."

"I'll do as you say, for sure!!"

"Secondly, you seem to be a mature young woman. You'll understand that I need your assurance that anything you read, see, or experience is for your eyes and ears only. You cannot tell friends, or anyone for that matter, what you've read, seen, or experienced. This may be hard, but you must keep it all between you and me."

"Okay."

"This is true in many types of work."

"You mean attorneys, doctors, priests, those kinds of people?"

"Yes, exactly. And, finally I would appreciate it if you would not tell people you're working with me. First it is nobody's business, and second, it is food for passing rumors and gossip. Wait until your project is complete and the case we're working on is closed. Can you do this for me?"

"Yes."

"Let's get to work. This week is the Coast Guard Festival in Grand Haven's Central Park. The craft show is Friday and Saturday. Please appear at my booth and I'll have an assignment for you. Plan on spending about four hours. You can stay longer, helping me sell my books, if you wish."

"Shall I be there at the start of the show or can I come early and help you set up your booth?"

"You can appear at any time, but let's make show-time when I'll expect you. Oh, and bring a notebook and a pen."

"Thank you, Mr. Searing."

"That's another thing. I appreciate the respect, but please call me Lou. I'll see you on Saturday morning. Thanks for your interest in investigating crime. Just remember that this is not exciting, but why should I say it? You'll see what I mean in time."

"See you, Lou. That doesn't sound right to call you, a respected adult, by your first name."

"Keep it up; it will feel natural after a meeting or two."

Sylvia's mother was smiling. "Thank you for helping Sylvia, Mr. Searing."

Lou looked at her and the two exchanged grins. Lou went home and took a nap.

✂

It was 11:30 when Sylvia called Lou from school. "I'm so sorry. I'm not to blame! Please know I had nothing to do with this, Mr. Searing."

"Whoa, slow down. I don't know what you're talking about."

"I'm afraid you'll think I caused this, but I didn't."

"Caused what to happen?" Lou asked. "Please explain."

"An article in the school paper says I'm working with you."

"Okay, things happen. Don't be upset. That doesn't bother me."

"My mom mentioned my working with you to her friend, Mrs. Arnold. Freddie Arnold, her son, is one of the editors of our school paper. He took off with the news. He didn't talk to me about this. He just printed it. I'm very sorry."

"All is well. I asked YOU not to share information. I should've made it clear to your mother."

"She's scared you will be angry and stop helping me." Sylvia was nearly in tears.

"There is no reason to be concerned. Now if she had said to her friend, 'My daughter is working with Lou, and he told Sylvia that so-and-so was an obvious suspect,' then I'm quite upset, very upset, but the article only mentions that you are working with me to fulfill the requirements of your vocations class without specifics; there's no harm done."

"I'm so relieved. Thank you for understanding."

"Now, what did you learn from this, Sylvia?" Lou asked.

"Uh, let's see. Do not say anything to anyone that you wouldn't say publicly."

"Yes, that goes for newspaper reporters, or to anyone who could use the information to embarrass you and that might lead to setting you up to be sued for libel or slander."

"For what?" Sylvia asked.

"There's another lesson for you. Look up the words 'libel' and 'slander' and define them for me when we meet on Saturday. Also look up what 'Off the Record' means, and on Saturday tell me when you would use such words."

"Okay. I'll do it."

"Now, tell your mom that I understand and all is well. She couldn't predict the consequences of talking to her friend. Which is another reason not to say something you wouldn't want to see in the newspaper or hear on television. I'm not upset with her. You learned a lesson and that's more important than a two-paragraph bit of news that's true. You might suggest to the editor that you be allowed to do a letter to the editor in which you don't deny the information in the article, but that this information was not supplied by you, and the newspaper did not verify the accuracy of the information before printing. If you wish, you could end it with it being an honor to work with Mr. Searing (not Lou in this instance) who is helping you meet the class requirements for your vocations class."

"Thanks, Lou. I'll do as you advise."

"One last question, please. Why didn't your mom call me?"

"She's scared."

"Another lesson. While we work together, you must always tell me what is on your mind. Don't ask anyone else to do it for you. I deal with people one on one. If you ever have something to say, tell me. I don't want to hear 'I guess I should have told you…' I'll decide if you erred, but you can't err in telling me the truth or in offering advice. These are lessons you would learn eventually. Always keep an open mind. Always question things, be analytical—the word 'Why' should be your best friend."

"Thanks, Lou. You're amazing."

"Not amazing, just experienced and a survivor. Now, I'm going to practice what I preach. Is your mom with you? If she is, please put her on."

Lou could hear, "Mom, Mr. Searing wants to talk to you."

"Hello, Mr. Searing. I am so sorry."

"No harm done. It provided lessons for Sylvia."

"I know I should've called to tell you of my mistake. I wasn't acting like a good parent. I didn't know my friend would tell her son."

"Everything is fine. Don't beat yourself up over this."

"I won't talk to anyone about Sylvia's experience. I've learned my lesson."

"Take a deep breath. Forgive yourself, and enjoy the rest of your day. Be thankful for your intelligent daughter. She's a rare and mature young woman, and she has a bright future. I've got to go."

"Thanks, Lou."

Within 10 minutes or so, Lou received a call from Dr. Zuckerman at Hackley Hospital.

"Thank you for calling, Doctor. What do you have for me or perhaps you're calling to ask a question."

"I'm calling you first, after talking with Elaine, who by the way gave me permission to talk to you. Jack's prognosis doesn't look good. He shows little sign of coming out of this coma. His breathing is labored. His heart is skipping beats. All of this can be treated, but these are signs his body is working very hard to sustain energy and to keep functioning."

"So are you saying you expect Jack to die?"

"Experience has taught me that a patient in this condition often doesn't live more than two weeks, three at the most. I will be talking more with Elaine soon. I'll be honest, but I'll try not to speak in a way that might cause her to give up hope."

"I understand. What can I do?"

"Pray, if that is meaningful to you. Put a prayer chain in motion."

"I'm sure Elaine has that under control. Jack's whole church is no doubt praying all day long for him to awaken."

"Lou, I have not told Elaine, but I want you to know that if Jack comes out of the coma and responds to treatment and therapy, it may be a long time before he returns to normal."

Lou took a deep breath. "He will be in and out of therapy for quite a while, is that what you're saying?"

"Pretty much. We can't predict what the body will do, but from experience he may not have a meaningful existence if he dodges death."

"Thanks for informing me. I appreciate your kindness."

"You're welcome."

✂

Lou asked Carol to join him on the shore. "It's early afternoon. We usually take evening walks," Carol reminded Lou.

"I know, and we may walk again this evening, but I need to talk to you and I want to talk on the shore."

"Absolutely. Let me get my deck shoes on," Carol responded, knowing something was going to be said that may be quite disturbing.

"I got a call from the hospital doctor responsible for Jack."

"Not good news?"

"He continues to be in a coma and if he eventually comes out of it, he'll likely be in therapy and rehab quite a while. This doctor is going to talk to Elaine and will continue to encourage her to hope for the best outcome."

"I'm very sorry, Lou."

"I could never successfully solve my cases without Jack."

Carol was alarmed at Lou's tone. "What will you do?" she asked.

"I'm not sure. Maybe it's time to draw the curtain on a long and satisfying career."

"This part of your life brings you so much joy. I can't imagine you not working to further justice."

"But, all good things must come to an end."

"Looks like it's time for your prayer du jour."

"Lots on my list; wishing for Jack to come out of this coma, for return to good health, and seeking a new direction for my life if Jack lacks the capacity to work with me."

"A lot on your plate, Lou."

"Yes, and ironically, it has nothing to do with solving a murder, unless it is the end of a passion to solve and write about the successful case. You know, on occasion I get asked why I write about murder. Murder is the wrong choice someone makes to deal with circumstances. I write about hope, about the power of love. I write my stories simple enough so that even people who don't like to read can find some enjoyment by reading."

"Why do you think murder mysteries are so popular?"

"I was asked that by a member of a club I spoke to. It was a good question and I've thought about it. I think people realize that it is something in our lives. Every newspaper, evening TV show, and news program covers serious crime. In the mystery book, justice prevails. I think of it as a reader saying, 'thanks for bringing some measure of justice while entertaining me.'"

"Looks like you have a good handle on it."

"I've had a couple of people ask me if I'm a Christian. I say I do the best I can. Then they asked, if I consider myself a Christian, why do I write about murder?"

"Have they opened their Bible?" Carol asked.

"Exactly. Lots of violence there. Cain and Abel, wars, stoning, feeding Christians to lions—the list goes on and on. Even the God of the Jewish people killed thousands by drowning in the Red Sea, making sure His people were taken care of. And then, of course, there is the murder of Jesus Christ. Taking of life appears almost normal. What is important is that justice be forthcoming. Love should conquer."

"Just tell them that they should open the Bible. Point out that Jesus says, 'Do not judge lest ye be judged'. When someone judges me, he simply tells me that when he or she judges, to put it mildly, he goes against the teaching of Jesus."

"Enough of this for an afternoon," Lou said, wanting to move on. "The writing is in the sand, if I may be dramatic, change is coming. I need to listen to the whispers of the Holy Spirit in the breezes off the lake. I just hope I can graciously accept whatever shore I walk along next."

Carol, the optimist replied, "All will not only be fine, but the future will be full of challenge and joy."

They shared a hug and then walked to their door. Turning around, they looked at peaceful Lake Michigan. Lou thought, *Whatever comes next will bring me joy.* He remembered the words of his Yoga teacher. "Repeat that you want to connect with God. Say the prayer of St. Francis, take many deep breaths, and then say, may I be peaceful and happy; may I be strong and healthy; may I be safe and free of harm; may I live in ease."

With those words in his mind, Lou entered their home, gave their golden retriever a pat on her head. He looked back at Lake Michigan and silently offered a prayer of thanks for having Carol in his life. She was clearly a loving spirit in human form. And, he offered prayers for Jack, Elaine, and the doctors and nurses who care for him.

Chapter TWELVE

The craft show murder was on track to be one of thousands of unsolved crimes. Detective Wheeler called Lou. "I just talked to Jake, the detective in Elyria. He said his murder is solved. When I asked for details, he said a woman walked into their police headquarters and admitted her husband committed the murder. Jake arrested the husband on the spot, locked him up."

"What was the motive and did the murderer know of the Farmington Hills Craft Show murder?" Lou asked.

"The motive should come out in court, but it appears to be greed. The answer to your second question is yes, he thought the method of operation made sense and he figured he wouldn't be caught."

"Then their case is closed as far as I'm concerned. Ohio's was a copy cat case, but that killer is not our criminal."

"I agree. Hey, how is your friend Jack?" Russ asked.

"He's still in a coma. The trauma doctor at the hospital wasn't upbeat. I got the feeling that death may be imminent."

"I'm sorry Lou."

"I can't solve murders without Jack. I'll probably retire. All good things come to an end."

"I hope not."

"I enjoy designing and crafting rosaries. I could give up writing a novel a year and craft religious items instead. I think people who pray with them will get as good a feeling with a rosary as they do now from reading a good mystery."

"Do what your soul guides you to do, Lou."

"Good advice, Russ. Thanks."

"Whatever you do, let's wrap up our case and put it in the case-closed file. I really think we need to get to Ohio and find Becky. I still think she holds the key to solving this. You've had a lot on your plate so I haven't suggested a trip to Ohio, but it's time if you are willing to go."

"For sure, I let that go. I'm back on it. Thanks for the firm suggestion."

✂

Lou was hauling wood to the fire pit on the beach, for the evening seemed perfect for a s'mores picnic. Word had gone out to the neighbors of a late-evening all-invited gathering at the Searing fire pit. Neighbors who enjoyed these beach fires with some refreshment would appear with beach chairs, blankets and an appetite.

Carol opened the back door and shouted, "Lou, come here, please."

He walked up to the porch and listened to Carol. "Elaine just called from Jack's hospital room."

"And…" Lou held his breath.

"Jack just came out of his coma. He recognized Elaine, and was asking what happened."

"Our prayers have been answered!" Lou exclaimed. "Whew, that's wonderful news."

"I knew you'd be happy. The doctor calls it a miracle."

"He probably says that to every family."

"I don't think so, Lou. The chaplain offered thanks for the miracle and spent more than a minute thanking God for Jack's being awake. And get this: Jack still has his sense of humor."

"How do you mean?"

"The first thing he said after recognizing Elaine was who had been licking his face!"

"She told him it had been a therapy dog. Jack asked, 'How much does the dog charge for his services?' Then Elaine said she broke down in tears of relief."

"Can he have visitors?" Lou asked.

"I presume so."

"Please call Elaine. Tell her that we're delighted and will be coming up to join in the celebration."

"I will. Shall we go right now?"

"One more armful of wood, and I'll be ready."

Lou and Carol entered Jack's room to find Elaine looking like a new woman. They stood on both sides of Jack's bed. Jack looked at Carol and cracked a smile. "Nice to see you."

"What a joy to see you awake," Carol replied.

"Jack, do you know who I am?" Lou asked.

"Sherlock Holmes," Jack replied. "Yes, Lou, I'm back from the dead."

"We're so thankful, Jack. So thankful."

"Got hit by a MAC truck, is what they tell me."

"You had us pretty worried, my friend," Lou said.

"I'll bet there is going to be some serious therapy and rehab in my future."

"It'll just be a time for you to slow down. We're so thankful you survived."

Lou talked to Doctor Westbrook outside of Jack's room. "What's Jack's prognosis?"

"He's doing better than I thought possible. All we can do is chart his progress and see what develops."

"How long will he be in the hospital?" Lou asked.

"Again, hard to predict. Just because he's awake and can answer questions doesn't mean he's out of the woods."

"Have the police been here to interview him?"

"Not yet."

"Thank you for all you've done and continue to do."

"You're welcome."

Sylvia appeared at Lou's booth at the appointed hour. True to her promise, she was dressed like a ninth-grader at a festival.

"Thanks for being here on time," Lou said.

"Sure. What do you want me to do?"

"Be super-sensitive to what you see and hear. Have a notebook, a pen, and a camera with you. First, please identify yourself to the show manager. Get her phone number in case we need to talk to her. I told her you would be working with me, so she should know of you."

"Okay."

"Once the show manager has met you, ask her for a list of all vendors. I also need access to vendor applications. We need more than the name of the vendor and their assigned space. Once we have applications on a computer, I'll give you your assignment."

Sylvia left the booth feeling like a deputized citizen in a Western flick. She located the show's manager, Violet Manning, and explained who she was. "My name is Sylvia Chappen. I live in Grand Haven and am working with Lou Searing. It would be normal for you to doubt me so if you wish I can call Mr. Searing on my cell and ask him to verify my information."

"I believe you. Lou explained you would be helping him. Let me have a little fun. Get him on the line."

"Mr. Searing. The show's manager, Violet Manning is here," Sylvia began. "I told her I was working with you. Would you assure her of that, please?"

"Okay, put her on."

"Hi, Lou. To start, there are child labor laws, you know."

"I'm aware, but I need to stretch the rules a bit. Sylvia has a ninth-grade vocations class, and she is learning about investigating crime. I have her mother's permission, as well as her teacher's blessing. She will not be in harm's way."

"Okay, I understand. Thanks for alerting me. Good luck."

Violet handed the phone back to Sylvia. "Okay, Sylvia, you have my attention."

"Thanks. Mr. Searing would like a list of all of your vendors and the booths to which they are assigned."

"Actually that's in our craft show pamphlet. Here's a copy."

Sylvia looked at the guide. "Will Mr. Searing have access to your data base if he needs more information than name and booth number?"

"All of that is in our computer here in the craft show information booth. Lou can have access to the applications, but I need to keep my computer here, and I don't want to forward the file to Lou."

"Ok, thanks."

Sylvia returned to Lou with the brochure. "What do I do now?"

"Sit in our booth and read the list of vendors for this show. I'm going to give you a list of vendors in Farmington Hills, Elyria, and in

Northview. I need you to compare all three lists and note any vendors who appear in all three shows, or in two shows."

"Okay." Sylvia put the three lists on a table and began comparing. Lou asked her to manage the booth if he needed to leave for any reason. Sylvia was a quick study, picking up quickly what she needed to do and say as a saleswoman for Buttonwood Press.

About two hours after the show opening, Lou wanted to walk a bit so he left Sylvia in charge. Within a minute, a middle-aged couple approached. "Is Mr. Searing here?"

"Not at the moment. He's at the show and should return soon. He just stepped away for a few minutes. Can I help you?"

"We have information about the case he is working on."

"What are your names? I'll have him contact you as soon as he returns."

"No names. We want to be a surprise."

When Lou returned to the booth about ten minutes later, Sylvia described his visitors.

"Wish I had a photo of them."

"Wish granted," Sylvia said, smiling.

"Granted?"

"See that man in the booth across from us and a couple to the right?"

"Yes."

"He looked like a nice guy. Earlier I had asked him if he would be willing to photograph anyone who stops to talk to us in our booth and anyone who might look suspicious. He said 'sure' so while I was talking to these people I saw him get in position and snap a photo or two. He forwarded the photos."

Lou looked at the image on Sylvia's phone and said, "I don't recognize either of them."

Lou told Sylvia to take over because he needed to speak with the show's manager. Violet was seated in the information booth when Lou arrived. "I need to speak with you privately."

Violet escorted Lou around to the back of her booth. "This will give us some privacy."

"I have just learned that an unidentified couple stopped here at my booth. I don't think they're dangerous, but they are people I don't know who want to see me about the murder."

"Thank you for letting me know. We do have a plan. Once you tell me to take action, I'll contact our security officers, who are in touch with the Grand Haven Police. If you wish them found, and they're within the park, they should be in custody within a few minutes. Again, thanks for telling me this, Lou."

"Let's leave this on standby. I'll let you know if I think finding this couple is important. Right now, it's good to know you have a plan of action, if needed."

Lou thanked Miss Manning and headed back to his booth. When he arrived, Sylvia was neither in the booth nor anywhere to be seen. He panicked. Every evil possibility passed through his brain as he looked in every direction. Then the man who had taken the photo of the couple approached Lou. "Sorry, I was supposed to tell you that the girl who is helping you had to use the bathroom, so I'm watching your booth. She should be back shortly."

"Thanks. We appreciate your helping us."

When Lou saw Sylvia walking toward his booth, he took a deep breath and said a silent prayer of thankfulness that she was okay.

"Hi, Lou. Why do I feel like I'm about to learn another lesson?"

"Because I have one for you. A small lesson, but an important one none-the-less."

"Okay, tell me."

"When we're working on a case, I must always know where you are, and vice versa: you must know where I am."

"I should have informed you I needed to visit a porta-potty. Is that the lesson? In my defense, I asked the nearby vendor to tell you."

"Yes, you did, but that person cannot necessarily be trusted. He could forget, or he might decide to leave to get refreshments, for example. You could have left me a note, or called me. When I came back and you weren't here, I panicked fearing you had been kidnapped."

"I got it! From now on, when we're on a case, you'll always know my whereabouts, and you'll always tell me your whereabouts."

"Yes. Now, I've told the show manager about the visitors and your photo. She has a system in place if we should sound an alarm. For the moment, she and her security staff will be on the lookout for the couple."

"So, we may be interrogating suspects before the day is over?"

"It's possible, but you'll not be involved. You're much too young and I'm sure the police chief wouldn't allow it and I will fully support him. I'll tell you all that I learn, but you can't be in on the questioning."

"I understand. Oh, I forgot to tell you; while you were away I sold about a dozen books. Several people asked if you were here today. I told them you were and that you would be willing to autograph the books for them."

"Good work. You haven't had time to match vendors with shared shows."

"That's right. If you're going to take over selling, I will give that assignment my full attention."

An hour later, Lou had sold several books, and there had been no word from security concerning the whereabouts of the couple who wanted to see Lou. Nor had he heard from Carol or Elaine regarding Jack.

Sylvia got Lou's attention. "I'm ready to tell you what I found after matching vendors at craft shows."

"Drum roll," Lou said.

"I used the Farmington Hills show as the master list. If a vendor was at the Farmington Hills show and at another, I used a green highlighter and made a note."

"Good." Lou glanced over the list and could see that Mackinac Island Fudge, Connie's Diamonds, John's Fire Pit Log-grabber, Bonnie's Embroidery, Barb Morse, Jerry Neikirk, and Cory Becker had been at all three shows.

"Sylvia, please find Connie's Diamonds booth at this show and check them out. It's possible the people tending the booth were the ones who came looking for me."

"Okay. I have my phone with me, and you have the number. I'm on my way to find Connie's Diamonds. I expect to be back in ten to fifteen minutes. You plan to stay here, correct?"

"Yes."

"Excellent. I'll be back."

Sylvia looked in the craft show directory. She saw that Connie's Diamonds was at B-81. She headed in that direction. The people in that booth were not the couple she was looking for, but she decided to watch from a distance, to see if something piqued her curiosity.

While Sylvia was gone, the couple looking for Lou approached his booth.

"Mr. Searing."

Lou looked up and saw the couple. "Can I help you?"

"Do you remember us?" the woman said.

"Can't say as I do. Should I?" Lou asked with instant realization that the couple was not a threat. "Excuse me for a minute; I need to place an important call." Lou called Violet and said, "Call off the search for the couple in the photo. Sorry, this is a case of mistaken identity."

"Thanks, Lou."

Lou returned attention to the couple. "Sorry. Where were we?" he asked. "Oh yes, you're surprised I don't recognize you. Are you a vendor at this show?"

"No, we are Mercy and Leonard Dickens. We were involved with the Coopersville Schools. You visited our school when you were Director of Special Education."

"I'm sorry. I could lie and say, 'of course,' but I must be honest."

"Well, it was thirty-plus years ago."

"It shouldn't matter. I should remember things like this."

"Anyway, it's good to see you," Mercy replied.

Len added, "Private detective? That's a long way from Director of Special Education."

"I suppose it is. I'm following my passions—putting my nose in other people's business and writing novels."

"While we're here we'd like to buy your last three books."

"Thank you. It was nice of you to stop and remind me of those special education days. I do have fond memories, but for the past twenty years I've enjoyed investigating and writing about the experiences."

"We enjoy craft shows, so we'll probably see you again."

"Wonderful, please stop."

The Dickens's moved on as Sylvia returned with a report about Connie's Diamonds for Lou. "That booth is not up. A neighbor said that Connie had taken ill and cancelled this show."

Lou concluded, "Well, not much excitement this afternoon. A couple of wild goose chases."

"Yes, but I learned a couple more lessons, and you sold some books."

✂

Lou couldn't put off his trip to Ohio any longer. For sure, it was on the front burner.

The address on the envelope that Lou photographed at Darlene's home appeared to be a home in Delaware, Ohio. Lou immediately made plans to go there in hopes of finding Becky. If she was in fact in Ohio, he couldn't understand why Darlene hadn't told him where Becky lived. Like many aspects of this investigation, that didn't make any sense.

Lou decided not to confront Darlene. That may happen down the line, but for now, finding the address for Becky was worth the trip.

Lou told Sylvia and Jack that he was going to Delaware, Ohio, to see what he could learn. He asked Carol if she wished to go with him. He was surprised when she said, "Sure, getting out of town for a day or two sounds good."

"Okay, we'll leave in the morning."

"That allows me time to arrange care for Sami and Sami II."

"I'll call Chief Kirk and explain that we will be gone for a day or two and that we will be staying at a Comfort Inn."

The next morning with overnight bags in the car, Lou prepared for the trip. He set the GPS for Delaware, Ohio, and with a light rain falling, Lou and Carol were on their way.

The trip was uneventful. Carol read her novel du jour. She spelled Lou on driving from time to time. The two worked together on a crossword puzzle. Carol read the clue, and Lou sometimes knew the answer. As noon approached the couple decided on fast food so as not to waste time in a restaurant booth. They pulled into Arby's for classic sandwiches, curly fries, and soft drinks. The final hours would be without wipers moving every few seconds.

About two o'clock, Lou and Carol saw the "Welcome to Ohio," sign. It had been a safe trip, and Lou and Carol were together enjoying each other's company.

✄

Sylvia asked Lou via text message if she could visit Jack. Lou thought it a great idea and Mrs. Chappen was willing to drive Sylvia to Muskegon so Sylvia could learn the role of Jack in solving these crimes.

Sylvia interviewed Jack and took copious notes for her report. Sylvia was amazed at how Jack accessed his database to find information for Lou.

Jack suddenly said, "I'm going to do something I have never done, but I think it should be done."

"What's that?" Sylvia asked.

"I sense Lou is being lured into a dangerous predicament. I'm going to call Chief Kirk in Grand Haven and ask him to intervene."

Jack called. "Good afternoon, Chief."

"Hello, Jack. It's good to hear your voice and on behalf of my staff, we're thankful for your recovery."

"Thanks, but I'm not out of the woods, yet. I still get headaches and have trouble moving around, but apparently my brain is functioning okay."

"Good. What can I do for you?"

"Lou has gone to Delaware, Ohio, in hopes of finding Becky Dawson, a suspect in the craft show murders."

"That's not like him, right?"

"He usually plans well, but I don't understand his just driving to Ohio without knowing if the person he wants to see is there."

"Maybe his age is getting to him?"

"He would normally have me research someone rather than going in blindly. But, for whatever reason, he's gone to Ohio and my gut tells me he is unknowingly walking into a fire."

"Why do you believe this?" Chief Kirk asked.

"Before my accident, I researched Becky and where she might be. I think I was on to something, but wasn't ready to tell Lou what I knew because I needed more information. As my memory keeps coming back, I recall Becky is tied to a group of dangerous people. I was ready to tell Lou that I was quite certain Becky Dawson murdered Stan Fedewa."

"Why had you reached this conclusion?"

"Stan was once a drug kingpin in southeast Michigan. Many heroin addicts depended on him to bring drugs into their world. When he came clean, he cut off hundreds from their supply. Addicts couldn't get their drugs from Becky who was their local supplier. So, there was a lot of anger to go around. The addicts were furious with Becky, and Becky was furious with Stan. I suspect her plan was to make Stan pay for shutting down the heroin flow into Michigan. Becky also was cut off as well. There was a price to pay. Some thought his coming clean meant he would report what he knew to police. If Becky killed Stan, it would show her buyers that the threat to tell the cops was removed. To show the displeasure of suppliers and addicts to Stan's cleaning up of the flow, he had to be punished. Murder was easy and quick, and a new kingpin could open up the market for their drugs of choice."

"Makes sense to me."

"As I was about to talk to Lou, I received a threat. If I continued to help Lou or the police I would risk having my days on earth numbered."

"Who threatened you?"

"I don't have a name nor a way to locate the person. The threat came in a phone call."

"Man or woman?" Chief Kirk asked.

"Woman."

"Any accent or vocal characteristic?"

"Midwest accent."

"Why were you picked? Why didn't they threaten Lou?"

"That's why I'm calling you. I think somehow she found out I was getting too much incriminating evidence against Becky. If they cut off my supply of information to Lou, the suspicion that Becky was a murderer would go away."

"So, someone forced you off the road."

"Yes. The vehicle had an Ohio license plate. I could see it in my rearview mirror as Ohio has plates on the front and back of the car."

"Why were you going south on Sheridan Road?"

"I knew I had to get to Lou, so I turned around and headed for Grand Haven. I didn't make it."

"Ok, now how can I help?"

"Becky lives in Delaware, Ohio. I see Lou, and I fear that Carol is with him, walking right into danger."

"Who would tip off the Ohio people about Lou being in the area?"

"Her sister, Darlene. Why? I suspect sisterhood. Family survival runs deep."

"Why can't you call Lou and warn him?" Chief Kirk asked.

"Because I think you should do the honors. My phone might be bugged."

"If that is true they already know of this conversation. And, the perpetrators will ambush Lou and Carol when they listen to this call."

"Right. Guess the brain isn't working as I would like. Either way, would you either call the Delaware, Ohio Police, or Lou, or both?"

"Sure. I'll let you know what happens."

Chief Kirk tried to reach Lou on his cell. After several rings there was no option to leave a message. Next he tried Carol's phone. Again, there was no answer and no option to leave a voice mail message.

Next Chief Kirk called the Delaware, Ohio, police. He explained who Lou and Carol Searing were, and that they were in the area, seeking a Rebecca Dawson. The officer who took the call did not know Rebecca Dawson. Chief Kirk said, "She supposedly lives at 1710 First St."

"Hold on," the officer said. Chief Kirk could hear people in the background.

"That isn't an address in the city of Delaware."

"Really? I have a photo of a letter addressed to Rebecca Dawson at 1710 First St. Delaware, Ohio. Where would it be delivered if no address?"

"It would be returned to sender."

"Thanks. Is there a First street?"

"Yes."

"Maybe one digit is wrong."

"Hold on. I think I know the confusion. That address is used as a way to communicate with a social service organization. They don't want their address given out so, when the post office employees see that address, they save the mail until the box owner picks it up."

"What is that organization?"

"That I don't know. I can give you the phone number for the local post office. You can call them and see if they can help you."

"Thank you." Chief Kirk called the post office number.

"This is David Kirk, Chief of Police in Grand Haven, Michigan. May I speak to the postmaster?"

"I'm the postmaster. What do you need?"

"I'm looking for a person of interest with a mailing address of 1710 First Street. Your local police tell me that mail addressed as such is held for someone from a service organization. Can you help me find the person I wish to speak with? Her name is Rebecca Dawson. She goes by Becky."

"The organization is Middle Grove Baptist Church. They have an outreach program for drug addicts. For obvious reasons, they don't want the public to know how to reach them."

"I understand."

"So, is there a Middle Grove Baptist Church in Delaware?"

"No, it's a fictitious name."

"So, I'm assuming you can't or won't tell me how to get in touch with someone in this organization?"

"You're correct; I can't reveal information."

"Please give me the P.O. Box Number."

"54."

"When someone picks up their mail, would you please tell the person to contact me?"

"Sorry again. This group demands absolute privacy."

"Can you at least tell me if someone from the organization stops in daily to get their mail?"

"Yes."

"What time of the day is the person picking up mail?"

"Usually around 1:00 p.m. We close for lunch, and when we open, the courier is often waiting."

"Thank you. May I ask for the same privacy? Please tell no one about my inquiry."

"Fine with me."

Chapter THIRTEEN

Chief Kirk finally managed to contact Lou by cell phone. He told him of Jack's call and what he had learned about Becky Dawson in Delaware, Ohio. Lou thanked the Chief. "I wasn't trying to be secretive. To me, it was necessary to drive to Delaware to see what I could learn, perhaps talk to Becky if I found her, and come on home. I guess it's much more complicated."

At 1:00 p.m., Lou and Carol were parked in the post office parking lot. Lou went to the front door where he joined several people waiting for the post office to open. Carol remained in their car writing down license numbers and noting the makes and models of the cars in the lot. She had her cell phone propped on the dash to take photos of people going into or out of the post office.

By the time the postmaster opened the door, six people waited to complete their mailing or pick up. Lou was only interested in someone taking mail from Box 54, and for fifteen minutes no one approached that box.

At 1:23, a young man, tall, tattooed, with long hair in a ponytail approached and used a key to open that box. He transferred mail to a small attaché, closed the box, and locked it. He left the post office, with Lou close behind. Seeing Lou, Carol knew this was their person of interest so she took a few photos.

Lou stopped the man. "Excuse me. May I have a moment of your time?"

"I'm in a hurry. What do you need?"

"I've heard that your organization does much good for people. Could I talk to you about this?"

The young man didn't want to seem uninterested or uncooperative, but at the same time, he obviously didn't want to talk to anyone.

"Um, our policy is not to seek attention. So, thanks for your interest, but please, no interview, no photos, nothing."

"Does your therapy take place in a church, a home, or public building?"

"Excuse me. I'm late for a meeting."

"Sure. Well, thanks for all you do to help others."

"Thank you," the man called over his shoulder.

Lou headed for his car while the young man got into a blue car driven by a woman.

"We're going to follow that car," Lou said as he climbed into the driver's seat. The blue car left the city and headed southwest on Route 36.

Lou maintained a distance so that the driver would not be suspicious.

Eventually, the vehicle with the young man pulled into the village of Ostrander, pulling over just past the main intersection. The young man got out and entered a storefront that seemed vacant. There were no lights, signs. He used a key to open the store, if that was what it was, and quickly closed the door. The driver of his car pulled ahead and parked in a 15-minute parking spot.

Lou and Carol parked a distance away where they could monitor all activity for two city blocks in all directions.

Eventually, a tall woman with a ponytail got out of the blue car and slowly walked to the vacant store. She walked up to the door, knocked, and waited to be let in.

"We seem to be making progress," Lou remarked.

"Really?" Carol did not understand.

"We have photos of the car and license plate. We have photos of people associated with an address claimed to be Becky's. And, the description of a possible suspect matches that of the woman who drove from the post office in Delaware to this vacant building in Ostrander. So, lots of progress!"

Because it was late August, it remained light until past 10:00. Lou sighed, "I suggest we check into our motel and call it a day."

"Fine with me," Carol said. "Are you going to check in with Sylvia, Jack, or Chief Kelly?"

"I'm okay. No need to do that."

When they got to the motel, they checked in, and the motel clerk handed Carol a sealed envelope. They received two keys to Room

13 on the first floor. The clerk wished them a good night's sleep. A continental breakfast would be served starting at 6:oo a.m.

They unloaded their car, inspected their room, took off their shoes and relaxed.

"What's in that envelope the clerk gave you?" Lou asked.

"Almost forgot about it. I put it in my purse."

Lou opened the message and read it out loud to Carol. "Listen to this: I guess I should welcome you to Ohio but in fact I encourage you to leave. I say this for your own good. We know why you're here, and your presence is alarming. Head home with my best wishes for a safe trip. Do not contact anyone or you'll have something in common with Jack Kelly, and you may not be lucky enough to survive."

"They're on to us," Carol said.

✂

After Lou read the note, he put aside any thought of being either a hero or a fool. He cancelled the room and told Carol they would do as the note said and head home. They quickly readied for their trip northwest. On the way out of Delaware with Carol at the wheel, Lou used his cell phone to call the police.

"Delaware Police. How may I help you?"

"Please put me through to your chief or if he or she isn't there, the assistant chief."

"What is this in regard to?"

"I am Lou Searing, assisting the Farmington Hills Michigan Police Department, investigating a murder there."

"One moment, please."

"Another name answered. Hello, this is Chief Arthur Weapon. How can I help you, Mr. Searing?"

"Did the receptionist explain the reason for my call?"

"Yes."

"The murder took place at a craft show. One suspect is a woman named Rebecca Dawson, or Becky. I came here because a letter for Becky had a Delaware, Ohio, postmark."

"This doesn't sound good," Chief Weapon said.

"Don't know how it sounds. I thought I was close to her when I received a message to get out of town or, in short, be killed."

"I can help you understand that. I don't know why Delaware was so lucky, but we became the home of a group of rebels. They are characters that intimidate townspeople."

"What do they do?"

"We were able to discover their tactics through undercover agents brought here from Denver. This group sends members, who number in the hundreds, ways to get money, legally as well as illegally to pay for a drug habit or to help their buyers get money to pay for drugs. They provide ideas for robberies where there is a low probability of getting caught. You mentioned a murder at a craft show. That is, believe it or not, one of their newest ideas."

"That makes sense. I've been monitoring this in the Midwest and have learned of two such crimes, one in Farmington Hills, Michigan, and one in Elyria, Ohio."

"Do you know Rebecca Dawson?"

"I haven't been able to confirm this, but rumor has it that she has been brought in to manage the national office. I have not seen her and I don't know much about her."

"Well, she's a suspect. Can you help me or the Farmington Hills Police?"

"Absolutely. What do you need?"

"First, let me know of any information you can find about her, and secondly once you have her in your sights, please let me know any movement of her or this organization. Also, I don't want her to know that I'm tracking her, but based on the message I got at my motel earlier, the organization knows of me and about my investigative partner, Jack Kelly. Lastly, please brief me if you hear of any plan or even a discussion of options for disturbing my investigation."

"I will do that, Lou."

"Thanks. Does this group own the town of Ostrander?"

"It might appear that way, but no, we coexist. The law has to be followed and it is."

"We're going to get on Route 23, then I-94 and head to Grand Haven, Michigan. Anything you can do to assure us a safe trip would be most appreciated."

"We'll do what we can, Lou."

"I sense this won't be the only time we'll talk. Thank you, Chief Weapon."

Lou and Carol forged on, stopping only for gas or a bathroom stop in a rest area. The "Welcome to Michigan" was a sign that brought some relief. For some reason, being in Michigan lowered their level of stress and anxiety.

In time, the Searings pulled into their drive. Lou turned off the ignition. He took a deep breath and offered a prayer of thanks for a safe trip with no life-threatening episodes. Carol was thankful their home appeared undisturbed. Sam and Sami II seemed happy to get pats, fresh food, and water. Maybe now, things would get back to normal.

✂

Unbeknownst to Lou, the city of Farmington Hills had offered a five thousand dollar reward for information leading to the arrest and conviction of Stanley Fedewa's killer. Calls came into a tip-line sponsored by the *Detroit Free Press*. Russ would scan the information and if a tip sounded reasonable, pass it on to Lou for his thoughts. Only one tip met that condition.

The message was, "I was walking my dog when she started to bark. I believed it was something in the distance because there was no visible scent, noise, or obvious movement nearby. I looked in the direction the dog was looking and I saw someone exit a vendor tent. There was only one person. I believe the person had long hair because when I saw the person run I could make out hair moving like a ponytail or long hair hanging loosely."

Russ asked Lou to look into it. Because this was a major clue that seemed legitimate, Lou made arrangements with the tip-line to interview the tipster.

Before leaving for Farmington Hills, Lou contacted Sylvia to explain where he was going and why he would go alone. Tip-line policy was that Lou did not know the name of the person, and they would meet in an enclosed room at the police station. The tipster was told that she would be questioned by a detective working with the Farmington Hills Police.

After introductions, Lou began, "You said the possible suspect had long hair in a ponytail or loose. What else can you tell me about the suspect's physical appearance?"

"She was slim. She ran from the vendor's tent, and I saw her run about a city block."

"Was she carrying anything?"

"Not that I could tell."

"Did she drive away from the park, or was she picked up by someone?"

"I didn't see her get in a vehicle, but seconds after I lost track of her, a car going fast drove past the park entrance."

"Can you describe the vehicle, even though you can't be certain she was in the vehicle as driver or passenger?"

"It was dark with no streetlights nearby. I would say it was a sports car of some kind, but I don't know the names of sports cars."

"When you learned the next day that a person had been murdered in the park, did you call the police with this information?"

"No."

"Because?"

"Because I was scared and didn't want to get involved. I also thought if I called the day would come when the murderer could come after me. I don't need major conflict in my life. I decided to leave that to the police."

"But you did call in this tip. Why is now different than the night of the murder?"

"Money. I need the money. Five thousand dollars would come in very handy about now."

"Ok, thanks for talking with me. The police have your name and contact information. I'm sure we'll be in touch with you one way or another."

"Do you know when that will be?"

"No, I have nothing to do with any of that. One more question. Did you tell anybody what you have told me?"

"I told my sister, but I swore her to secrecy. I trust her and am certain she wouldn't tell a soul."

"Have you been threatened by anyone?"

"No, do you expect I will be?"

"No, just part of my questioning. One more question, please. How old would you say this woman was?"

163

"I would say in her twenties or thirties."

"And, how sure are you that the person was a woman? In this day and age, anybody could have long hair."

"I feel quite certain the person was a woman, but I wouldn't swear to it."

"Here's my card," Lou said, handing the woman his business card. "If you have any more information that would give credibility to the suspect being a woman with long hair, and in her thirties, please contact me. Please feel free to call the Farmington Hills Police Department and ask for Detective Russ Wheeler."

"I hope I'm awarded this money."

"So do I. Thanks for calling in the tip and for talking with me."

Lou knew Russ was away from the station so he called him to tell him what he had learned. "Suspect might be female, 30 years old, slim, with long hair. The tipster saw a woman run from a vendor's booth late at night."

"Thanks. This is the first indication that the suspect is a woman who acted alone."

"Just a step forward," Lou replied.

"I don't have to remind you that there are so many holes in this report."

"I know. It could have been a guy with a disguise, could be the wrong vendor booth. We only have one person's 'I think' but that's more than we've had to-date. At least it's something to go on. Were there other responses to the reward?" Lou asked.

"There were about a dozen. The majority were crank calls , and the rest were worthless to us because of inconsistencies between the tips and known facts."

Chapter FOURTEEN

Russ called Lou. "I've got a tip for you."

"A guy named Rod Hastings was picked up in Royal Oak. We have information that ties him to Becky."

"Is he confined or free?"

"He's in custody. Royal Oak Police will be working with us and assures us that a judge would not consider his release until we have the chance to question him about your case."

"Thanks. I hope Royal Oak Police get as much information about him as possible."

"We work well together. I'll be going to Royal Oak to question him. You are in Grand Haven now, correct?" Russ asked Lou.

"Yes. I could be in Royal Oak in four hours."

"I really want to question him sooner."

"I understand," Lou replied. "You go ahead. I've plenty to do here at home.

I wouldn't be surprised if this guy were a bona fide sociopath."

"I'll call with information or you can call in a few hours for an update."

✂

Russ asked Rod Hastings if he knew Becky Dawson

"Yeah, I know her. Was married to her."

"You abused her?"

"One person's abuse is another's consensual roughing around."

"Consensual?"

"Yeah, she loved being roughed up."

"Did you kill Stan Fedewa?"

"Who is this Stan whatever you said?"

"Fedewa. He was murdered in the craft booth where Becky worked.

"Oh yeah, that good-for-nothing jerk. No, I didn't kill him."

"Did Becky supply you with drugs?"

"Yes. Everybody has a dealer, and she could get powerful drugs at low cost."

"She couldn't supply you when Stan stopped dealing. How did you react to that?"

"She said her supplier stopped dealing in drugs and that her source dried up. I was not happy. A lot of people were not happy."

"So, the drugs you needed couldn't be gotten. Somebody has to pay the price for you not getting your cache."

Rod was silent, looking down.

"The way I see it, she had to pay the price," Russ reasoned. "So you punished her by physically abusing her. It doesn't look good for you."

"Listen, I didn't kill no supplier."

"Did you ever meet Stan Fedewa?" Russ asked.

"Yeah, I went to the golf course to get some drugs. He pulled up while I was with Becky."

"Describe him."

"Big guy, cigar. He knew I wasn't playing golf or on staff, so he threatened me."

"Threatened you how?"

"He yelled, told me to dry out. He was just asking for it."

"So, you're saying you made it your business to make Fedewa pay for his dropping out of the drug business."

"He didn't like my way of letting him know that if he didn't find the drugs, he'd be beaten pretty severely."

"So, you killed him."

"No way. I can get drugs in prison, but no women in prison, no freedom. I might not be the sharpest knife in the drawer but I'm not into prison. It's not my idea of fun."

"So, you admit to abusing Becky," Russ summarized.

"Depends what you mean by abuse. I grabbed her, pushed her, that kind of thing, but to me that's not abuse. You on the other hand, based on some lies told to you, want to call it abuse. I can't prove you're wrong, but I know that I'm right."

"And, you warned the supplier, Fedewa, if he didn't get back to dealing drugs, he'd regret it."

"Yes. I did threaten him."

"So, who killed him?"

"How would I know?"

"Becky might kill him, because with him dead, you'd be off her case. How can she buy from a dead man?" Russ suggested.

"It's your job to find out who murdered the guy, not mine," Rod said sarcastically.

"True, but your case could be looking up if we verify that you cooperated."

"I don't play those games. I didn't kill anybody, and I certainly don't know who killed the 'cigar guy'."

Lou called Russ who didn't pick up because he was questioning Rod. He called back as soon as he could.

"Yes, Lou. You called."

"Just touching base. Are you learning anything?"

"I don't get a sense that this guy killed Stan, but I latched onto a new theory."

"If you're busy now, you can tell me when you have a moment."

"I'm taking a break from questioning Rod. I'll tell you now. I'm thinking the killer most likely is Becky. The following might make sense. Follow me. A motive could be Stan no longer provides her with drugs, which means she can't supply Rod. So, Rod abused her. Becky figures if Stan were dead, Rod couldn't expect her to have drugs. So, Becky lures Stan back to the booth that night. He doesn't see her as a threat and isn't surprised when she enters the booth."

"A likely scenario," Lou admitted.

Lou thought the time was right to involve Sylvia. He invited her to go with him to Pontiac, Michigan, the county seat for Oakland County to review reports. She accepted his invitation and the next morning, they were on their way.

Lou suggested some coffee and chocolate chip cookies at the Coopersville McDonald's. Sylvia thought it a good idea but chose a healthier parfait and bran muffin. Once in the car and on their way, Lou spoke about the case.

"I think this is a good time for you to get involved. We'll be reading police reports and maybe interviewing some people, looking at the scene of the crime. I can give you a more thorough briefing on the way down."

"Just so I won't mess up again, my role is to listen, watch, think, and note what I think is important. Right?"

"Exactly. On occasion, I might ask if you have a question or a thought, but otherwise, you are an observer. I expect your contribution mainly during our discussion on the way home."

"Okay, bring me into the case."

For the next hour or so, Lou brought Sylvia up to speed, telling her just about everything he knew about Becky, which wasn't much. "I think the motive for the murder was drugs. Stan used to be a drug kingpin in Oakland County. Becky was one of his suppliers, and she also took drugs. I learned that the county has a file on Becky. I'm referring to arrests, petty crimes, shop-lifting, burglary, that sort of thing. To save time, I have asked the county sheriff to make available police reports, forensic reports, and witness interrogations. So, I hope to enter a conference room to find a stack of files. We will go through them, looking for anything that piques our curiosity."

"Thanks, Lou."

Lou's cell phone rang. He noted the caller and handed the phone to Sylvia asking her to handle it.

"Hello. This is Sylvia. Mr. Searing is driving now. May I help you?"

"Yes, you can. I'm Laura James, a feature writer for the *Grand Haven Daily Tribune*. My editor has asked me for a human interest story about you and Mr. Searing. Would you and Mr. Searing consent to interviews and a photo of you together?"

"Hold on. I'll ask Mr. Searing."

"Take your time."

Sylvia told Lou of Laura's request. After a moment's thought, Lou said, "Tell her 'thank you' for thinking of us. I would be glad to be interviewed, but I ask her to wait until this case is solved. It makes for a more interesting story, and it keeps the public's attention off the case."

Sylvia told Laura of Lou's response. "That's fine. Thank you, Sylvia."

"You're welcome. I'll have to ask my parents for their consent. I can't imagine them objecting, but I can't answer you without their okay."

"Understood. Thank you and enjoy your day."

Two hours later, Lou pulled into the county sheriff's office in Pontiac. "Let's hope we get some information that's helpful in solving this case."

"I have a good feeling about it."

"That's a good attitude, Sylvia. Being positive is an important trait."

Lou and Sylvia entered the sheriff's office, signed a visitor log, and asked to speak with Deputy Lonzo, who's handling the craft show murder. "He knows I'm coming to review files," Lou explained.

"Oh, yes. We've been expecting you. The files and reports you requested are in the conference room. Please go right, walk down the hall. The conference room's the third door on your left."

"Thank you. You will tell Deputy Lonzo that we're here?"

"Yes, definitely. Can I get you something to drink?"

Lou said, "I would like black coffee."

"I'd like chocolate milk," Sylvia said.

"Oh, that's not an item on our refreshment list."

"Okay. I'd like water."

"Coming up."

Lou captured a glance from Sylvia. Both smiled. Lou seemed to say, "Hey, she asked, and you were honest."

Sylvia said, "Sorry, Lou. That was a bit childish. I know, water it is. Do you have any suggestions for delving into these files and reports?" Sylvia asked. "I'd like someone to brief me of the basics so I'll have some idea of what happened."

"I agree; excellent suggestion."

Lou requested Deputy Lonzo to introduce the records regarding Rebecca Dawson. Mr. Lonzo entered the room and listened to Sylvia's request for a summary.

"Suspect is Rebecca Dawson, age 26. Single, no primary residence spent some time with an estranged sister. She's stayed at a homeless shelter, at a home for abused women, and spent some time living in what we might call a commune. We have no record of friends. We have no evidence of weapons. She committed crimes alone. There have been no accomplices in her crimes; however, her former husband might have been involved. She's been picked up on the street, primarily for buying or selling drugs. To our knowledge, once she got into the drug scene to support her addiction, she got into selling. To maintain her addiction, she commits petty crimes. We were able to inspect the apartment where she slept on occasion. The people who lived with her were druggies. By the way, within two days of my inspection of the property, the apartment was evacuated. Gone. Residents, we were told were six females and one male. Out of the women, only one seemed willing to talk, but she didn't show up for an interview. Any questions?"

"You've given us an excellent summary," Sylvia said.

Lou added, "Yes. Thank you. With that information, we'll delve into all of this paperwork and will undoubtedly have a few questions."

"I plan to be at my desk all day." Deputy Lonzo left them to their work.

Lou and Sylvia pondered an eighteen-inch pile of reports. Lou spoke, "Let's get going on these files. When you're finished with a file, put the folder on a pile in front of you. I'll do the same. I suggest you take a couple packs of sticky notes. When you have a question or an insight, jot it on a sticky note and when we are finished reviewing the contents of these files, we'll discuss what we've highlighted."

"Looks like this will take a day short of forever," Sylvia said, looking forlorn.

"It's a lot but we won't be reading every file, and in many cases, a file won't be relevant. Let's get started. You'll see how quickly this goes."

"But what am I looking for?"

"Red flags."

"What does that mean?"

"Something that you see or read that just doesn't make sense or something we've not heard that we need to look into. You'll figure it out. For example, you will find a drawing of the crime scene. My guess is that we won't find that helpful."

"I see."

The receptionist appeared in the conference room. "Miss Sylvia, here is chocolate milk. The Chief said we should do whatever we can to assist you in solving our case. I quote, 'If she wants chocolate milk, she gets chocolate milk.'"

"Thank you very much," Sylvia said delighted. "My request was childish but I was being honest. I would like chocolate milk so I said it. On second thought, I should have realized chocolate milk would be an inappropriate request. Please thank the Chief for me."

The woman smiled. "Will do."

As they began looking through folders, Lou spoke up. "Sylvia, there may be photographs that aren't suitable for you to see."

"I can handle it."

"I'll decide."

"Of course. I understand."

They spent the next three hours reading, placing sticky notes on an occasional page. Lou broke the silence when he said, "When you get to the collection of evidence, here is a report you should read carefully. I refer to the contents of a purse, for example."

Lou's suggestion was timely because Sylvia was about to study what forensic experts had itemized from Becky's purse. There were typical things like pens, calculator, gum, some makeup, and money, change and bills. Sylvia's curiosity led to her reviewing each paper bill. She and Lou shared a lighted magnifying glass. She looked at each side of the bill. For the first ten or so bills, they saw nothing out of the ordinary. Then, mixed in with bills was a stub from Becky's paycheck from the golf course. Using a pen, someone had written "Spend this wisely. No more paychecks unless issued and mailed from Hell."

Sylvia excused herself and told Lou where she was going. "Whoa, you can't go into the evidence room."

"I can read all of these reports that mention evidence but I can't look at it? I don't understand."

"It would be fine with me but only authorized personnel can enter."

"Can I be with an escort? I'd like to see an evidence room."

"You can ask Deputy Lonzo. If he will go with you, who am I to interfere?"

"If he says, no, don't push it."

"I know what to do. Thanks."

Deputy Lonzo and Sylvia walked into the evidence room where Sylvia was hoping to find Becky's calendar.

Everything was in plastic bags. A sign on the door of the evidence room warned visitors to wear sterile gloves when handling any item. She complied and lifted the calendar into her hand. She opened the bag and removed the calendar. She leafed through it, focusing on the weeks prior to and after the murder. A day before the murder she read, "I can't take any more of this jerk. Expect a commotion at the Farmington Hills show. Someone will experience Karma." Sylvia put a sticky note on this page. She returned the calendar and notebook to the evidence bag. She removed the gloves, signed out, and after thanking Mr. Lonzo for his help, returned to the conference room.

"Well, that was interesting."

"What's interesting?" Lou asked.

"The place is an organizer's heaven!"

"Yes. It has to be. While you were gone, I didn't have a nibble on my baited hook."

Over the next couple of hours, Lou and Sylvia studied files and discussed items with sticky notes; but when it was time to leave, they really didn't know much more than when they went in. Lou found the note on the pay stub interesting and the calendar notation, but neither implicated Becky in murder.

They returned to Grand Haven disappointed.

Chapter FIFTEEN

The next day Lou called Jack who was now home. A visiting nurse made sure Jack was comfortable and getting the therapies and visits from specialists that were part of his rehabilitation plan.

"How are you doing, friend?" Lou asked.

"Getting along okay, I guess, given the alternative."

"Do you have any memory of the accident?" Lou asked.

"A little comes back to me each day."

"What caused you to leave the road?"

"That isn't clear to me yet."

"A deer running across the road?" Lou suggested.

"I don't remember."

"Did someone run you off the road?"

"I'm sure that's what happened."

"The police report notes that you drove off the road as your car was headed south. I can't figure out why you were going south."

Jack appeared to think, closed his eyes trying to pull up a response to Lou's question. Jack didn't say anything, he just shook his head.

"Why weren't you wearing a seat belt? If anyone in the whole world would have his seat belt buckled, it would be you."

"I can't imagine that, either. Who said I wasn't wearing the belt?" Jack asked.

"It was written in the police report."

"Hmmm, it could have snapped when I hit the tree."

"No. The report indicates that the belt was not on your waist on impact."

"Got me. Let me know once you figure it out."

"Have you had any more threats?" Lou asked.

"What threats?"

"When you visited me before your accident, you said you had been threatened."

"I don't recall."

Lou's phone rang. He saw Sylvia was on the phone.

"Hold on, Jack. I've got to take this call."

"Call me later, Lou. I'm getting a headache. I need to rest."

"Sure. Will be in touch."

"Hello, Sylvia, what have you got?"

"I don't know if you've heard, but I just learned that the State Police in the Upper Peninsula have reported a theft at a craft show. This one is near Munising."

"Who told you about this?"

"That news reporter in Grand Haven. She saw it come over the wire and wanted me to know."

"I should be jealous? People with big news now go through my 9th grade assistant."

"She said she called your home phone which was all she had. No one answered so she said she didn't leave a message and called me at school. No need to be jealous, it makes me feel good that I'm the one who gets to brief you for a change."

"I'll call to see if there are any similarities, but I doubt it."

This was the first time that Lou missed Jack's wisdom. It was at times like this when the two men would put their heads together and try to make sense of what made no sense.

Then Lou called the Munising Police to inquire about the murder. "I'm Lou Searing. I'm assisting Detective Russ Wheeler of Farmington Hills Police in solving the craft show murder about a month ago."

"Okay and you want information about our case?" Detective Marie Hathaway of the Munising Police asked.

"Yes."

"How so?"

"We think the killing was not the original plan, that the motive for the crime was robbery."

"The vendor surprised the thief?" Lou asked.

"Yes, different mode of operation. I said there were no witnesses, but I misspoke. We do have someone who has come forth with some information. Would you like to interview him?"

"Yes, please. I can get what I need over the phone."

✄

Lou called the number given to him by Marie Hathaway.

"Willie Proctor, correct?" Lou began. "I understand you were at the Pictured Rocks Craft Show last weekend. Correct?" Lou asked.

"Yes, I was there as a tourist. I'm a crafter too, so I like to see what others do in their spare time."

"What time did you witness the crime?"

"I would say around 7:00 in the evening."

"And the show closed at 5:00, is that right? Please tell me what you saw."

"I've already made that clear in the report I gave to police. I have nothing to add."

"I want to hear the details from you."

"Okay, the sun wouldn't set for a few more hours, and I was walking through the park. All the vendor booths were closed with zippers. I saw somebody open a booth and enter, pulling the zipper down. For all I knew, it was his booth."

"Then what happened?"

"About five minutes later a vehicle pulled up in front of that booth. The driver got out, unzipped the northwest corner zipper and entered the booth area."

"Did you hear anything, see anything, sense anything was amiss."

"A minute or two later, the man from the car came out of the booth at the same corner and put something in his car. He went back in and came out maybe three times. I figured it was his booth, and he was simply bringing additional crafts or taking some away."

"Did you take any photos?"

"No."

"You didn't hear or see anything to indicate a struggle?"

"Not a sound, not a ripple in the covered booth."

"Then what happened?"

"He drove away."

"Can you describe the vehicle?"

"It was an SUV. They all look alike these days. I think it may have been blue. It didn't stand out in any way."

"And, the man?"

"Normal guy, medium height and weight. He was just a middle-aged man. Nothing special."

"Nobody in his car?"

"Not that I could tell. Remember, I wasn't thinking crime, much less murder. I was just walking, enjoying the scenery in the park. If someone had said, 'Pay attention because a murder is going to happen,' I would have noticed as much detail as possible."

Lou called the Munising detective after interviewing Willie. "What was the craft of the man who was robbed?" Lou asked.

"I think it was jewelry-making."

"What is Willie's craft?"

"I don't know."

"Find out and if it is the same craft as the victim, prepare for an arrest warrant."

"Evidence or gut?"

"Gut, but making its way to evidence."

"Why would you think this?"

"Nobody just takes a walk enjoying the scenery in a craft show area after the show closes for the day."

"Because…"

"For one, there's no scenery. Two, what's to enjoy about looking at a bunch of enclosed canvas huts? My guess is if you take his comments re car, personal description, whatever he says he saw, if you take just the opposite, you would be describing him."

"You've got a good point there, Mr. Searing."

"I think the thief is your cooperative witness."

"Why would he come forward wanting to help?"

"So, he could control the investigating. This assures he would be a good guy for being willing to help, but at the same time steering the investigation away from him."

"Interesting. But how can you be so sure?"

"I can't be sure."

Detective Hathaway called Mr. Proctor. "Would you please come to the police station? We need to take fingerprints. We'll also need your driver's license and make and model of your car."

"Why on earth do you need this? I'm cooperating by sharing what I saw and now it sounds like I'm a suspect. Leave me alone!" Willie slammed the phone down on the desk. He was angry and could tell he was losing control, just as he had done on other occasions when he felt wronged.

Detective Hathaway told Lou what Willie had said. "Pick him up, Detective."

"You think so?"

"Can't do any harm. He's a legitimate suspect."

"Detective Hathaway advised her chief to pick up Willie Proctor. The chief was reticent to do so, but he agreed and sent a squad car to find Willie. He didn't live in Munising so finding him would be a challenge, but it only took one call to a motel in Munising to verify that Willie Proctor was a guest.

Unfortunately, the police car arrived with sirens blaring and lights flashing. Willie lost it, grabbed his gun and prepared for a confrontation. Two police cars were stopped outside Room 30, and six officers exited the vehicles with revolvers drawn. One officer using a bull horn said,

"Willie Proctor. Come out with your hands up, NOW!"

Willie turned on the television, turned the volume up and went into the bathroom, where he knocked out the back window. He slipped out and with a loaded gun in hand, he began running, but instead of finding a wooded area, he ran down Superior Street and kept running south on US 28.

When police broke the door down and found an empty motel room, the officers fanned out searching for Willie. A call to 911 had reported a man with a gun running south on Route 28. Within a couple of minutes, Willie was spotted heading down railroad tracks. The police pursued and soon Willie was arrested.

As promised, Lou contacted Sylvia to explain what had happened. Lou asked Sylvia to call Jack and explain what had happened in Munising. He would call Russ and report.

"Russ, I am fairly certain that the Munising robbery is not connected to our case. The Munising Police have arrested a suspect, Willie Proctor. I'll see what I can learn about Proctor. I'll check the data base, and I'll check in with you tomorrow."

Carol called Lou into the kitchen. "I forgot to mention that Elaine Kelly called. She wanted you to know that Jack is making great strides in remembering things. The doctors are calling his recovery outstanding."

"That's wonderful news."

Sylvia called Lou and asked for permission to call Mr. Kelly.

"Absolutely. You will enjoy him."

Sylvia, with cell phone, called Jack. He answered. "How is my replacement doing these days?"

"You can't be replaced, Mr. Kelly. I'm watching Lou struggle without having you on the case. I guess you really don't appreciate what you have till you don't have it."

"Oh, I think Lou appreciates my contribution and I also know he's enjoying having your help. He's also enjoying teaching you the ins and outs of investigating. You are most fortunate to be learning from Lou."

"Believe me, I know that. I asked Mr. Searing if I could call you. He gave me permission."

"You can call me anytime you want. How can I help you?"

"Just wondered if you had thoughts about the craft show murders."

"Serial killer. This is not copy-cat killing. There's a theme going on here. The key is to find out the common link as to who and why killing these people brings satisfaction. I'm sure you and Lou have focused on common characteristics between the victims."

"You mean like, they all sell art work or jewelry."

"Exactly."

"If they all sell or make the same craft you could compile a list of all vendors who sell that craft so they can be alerted so they can choose which shows to attend in the future."

"Thanks, Mr. Kelly."

"Jack's my name. Thank you for your respect, but we're part of Lou's team and he doesn't expect formality."

"Oh, Jack. I'm thankful you are feeling better."

Sylvia's mother drove to the Grand Haven State Park, because Sylvia wanted to take a walk along the Lake Michigan shoreline. She sat on a piece of driftwood. She asked for wisdom, clear thinking, and perhaps making sense of this case.

She thought, *Obviously the murders have something to do with the craft show world. It seems obvious that solving these murders will be determined to be people inside the craft show world. This should not be rocket science. Is there a pattern that would reveal the killer, the motive? I need to find the pattern.*

Sylvia went home, took out her notebook and made columns for possible patterns. The columns were labeled vendor name, sex of vendor, product selling, possible motive. She spent more than an hour filling out the chart, but in doing so she couldn't find a pattern. It looked to be three separate crimes with some common features, but she couldn't discern the pattern that she had hoped would appear.

Chapter SIXTEEN

Lou and Sylvia drove to Farmington Hills to meet with Detective Russ Wheeler. After much discussion, it was the consensus of the three that the FBI needed to be brought in. Russ requested assistance from the Detroit office. "We have a suspect who is in Delaware, Ohio. We need to find her and talk to her."

"I will transfer you to Agent Sally Harrison."

Sally took the call and asked, "Do you suspect her of murder?"

"Yes. She was the last to see the victim. She disappeared immediately after the crime and we can't seem to find the missing link to put on the cuffs, if she is in fact guilty."

"Where is she now?"

"We have a mailing address for her which is on First Street in Delaware, Ohio. My colleague, Lou Searing, went down there to see if he could locate her. He was threatened with his life if he didn't leave immediately, so he did. Lou talked to the police chief in the town where an office is located which is linked to her, but without any credible evidence of illegal activity he couldn't intervene, nor could the local police."

"Let me check our data base. You said her name was Becky Dawson?"

"That's right, Rebecca Dawson."

"Any aliases?"

"None."

"Well, she is in our data base. References are for drug trafficking. She appears to be a loner. We don't have an address for her."

"It's frustrating," Russ replied. "We know where she is, but short of breaking into an office, we can't move forward."

"Thank you for consulting us, Detective Wheeler. We will find her and advise you of her whereabouts, and we'll also provide her to you for questioning."

"Thank you, Agent Harrison."

Within a day, Russ Wheeler received a call from FBI Agent Harrison. "We found your suspect. She is affiliated with an organization called Middle Grove Baptist Church, and she resides at a temporary shelter for homeless women. Local police said she is a drug abuser, but she hasn't been arrested. These are phone numbers for the organization and the shelter."

Russ passed the information to Lou, asking him to follow up.

Lou called the shelter. "May I speak with Miss Dawson?"

"I will transfer you to her room."

"Thank you."

"Hello," a woman answered.

"Is this Miss Dawson?"

"Yes. Who's calling?" Becky asked.

"This is Lou Searing, a fellow crafter. I sell my Michigan-based murder mysteries at craft shows."

"I enjoy your books. I love mysteries! I assume you're calling about Stan Fedewa?"

"Yes, I am. You left town so we couldn't find you after Stan's murder."

"I got out of town as fast as I could. I knew I would be suspect number one, and I didn't want the trouble that comes with a murder investigation. But I knew you or someone would eventually find me. And you have."

"As far as I'm concerned, you are the most important person in my investigation."

"Well, now you have me. Ask what you want."

"I might as well lead with the highest priority question. Did you kill Stan?"

There was a pause. "I'm going to be honest with you, Mr. Searing. I'm a pretty good liar, but because of the respect I have for you, I know you will see through any lie, so I'll save you time and energy and get right to the honest answer."

"Thank you," Lou replied.

"The answer is I did not kill him, meaning I didn't inflict the wound that led to his death. I did send a report to all of our subscribers explaining how to carry out petty thefts. I wrote what we call Bulletin #7. In this bulletin I explain that craft show vendors are easy targets for theft. I cite the lack of security, the fact that booths are rarely locked up, that vendors often don't take their valuables home for the night, and the shows are often in parks. The members of our group might wish to carry out the steps to take valuable wares. While murder is not recommended, we tell our members that if killing another is needed to successfully carry out the heist, there are steps and procedures to follow."

"So, you provide to your members a 'How to…' in terms of craft show thievery."

"Yes."

"Someone practiced on your partner, Stan."

"Unfortunately."

"Do you know specifically who killed Stan?"

"No. But, I'm sure it's one or more of our more than 400 subscribers."

"Can you give me a list of your subscribers?"

"I can, but I won't."

"Can you send me the bulletin explaining how to steal from vendors?"

"I can, but I won't."

"I can understand that you probably don't wish to divulge that information, but I'm sure I can get assistance from a judge. And your decision not to cooperate by withholding information necessary to solve this crime will be something that should concern you."

"This is the thanks I get for giving you information?" Becky asked.

"I appreciate your information and cooperation. A man has been killed. Justice needs to follow."

"You may find justice, but when word gets out of what I told you, I'm dead."

"Literally?"

"Yes, literally. You simply do not turn on a member of the organization."

"I understand."

"And, more importantly for you, once the word gets out that you've found the killer and are responsible for the person going to prison, you'll need to look over your shoulder for the rest of your life. To hundreds of people you will be public enemy number one."

"I understand. Thanks for talking to me and answering my questions. Call me if you think of anything else that might help us find Stan's killer."

"Will I get a visit from the police?"

"Now YOU can look over YOUR shoulder every minute, because you don't know what action I'll take."

✄

Lou called Cory Becker once again. "I think I'm onto something and I need your help. I'm fairly certain that two women were involved—the killer and an accomplice. Let me put words into your mouth. Judy Gentilozzi was the woman who was angry and another woman was angry as well, but you couldn't identify her. Correct?"

"Yes."

"Was any other woman in the show making threatening comments about Stan?"

"Not that I recall."

"I had a thought that might prove helpful. It occurred to me that the killer may have stayed in an RV on the site. Do you know of any women who stayed in an RV during non-show hours?"

"No, but you might talk to Johnny Facely, a vendor from Illinois. He travels to several shows in the Midwest."

"Does anyone travel with him? I refer to a wife, a daughter, or any female?"

"I think his wife works his booth. But he is not your killer, Lou. I know people are shocked when seemingly innocent people kill, but this family is full of peace and love. They are the last people who would ever commit murder."

"I'll find where their booth was located and where their RV was assigned. Anything else, Cory?"

"No, and finally, I'm not thinking about the case every waking moment, which is a good thing."

"Healing takes time. You'll be okay."

Lou found the application for J. Facely. Attached was a form for overnight parking. He called Johnny and introduced himself. Lou was gratified to hear Johnny was familiar with him and his books.

"In the murder of the vendor, Stan Fedewa, I suspect the killer may also be a vendor, and may have spent the night at the park. I'm looking for a woman, a tall woman. Did you see anyone in the camping area fitting that general description?"

"A woman had a camping slot two down from us," Johnny replied.

"Did you notice anything strange?"

"I'm not a good sleeper. I seem to take a series of naps all night long. I thought it strange that this woman left in her car and was gone about thirty minutes. When she came back, I thought it odd that she went behind her RV."

"You were in what slot?" Lou asked.

"I can't recall. I'll need to look in my files. Is it important for you to know the number?"

"Yes. Please look."

A few minutes later, Johnny came back on the line. We had RV Slot 29."

"So this woman would have had number 27 or 31," Lou concluded.

"Yes."

"Was she alone or with her family or anyone for that matter?"

"I can't help you there. If you had a photo, I could say whether it was the vendor who parked near me in the camping area."

"Thank you, Mr. Facely. You've been very helpful. I'll be in touch."

Lou thumbed through the applications until he found the vendor who was assigned RV Slot #31 in Farmington Hills. Her name was Barb Morse, and her address was listed as Cincinnati. Lou called Russ and suggested that Barb might be a key player in the case. "Let's find Barb and talk to her," Russ directed.

"Please do this without me. You are the law and are more credible," Lou advised. "I'd rather she didn't learn how I came to accuse her."

"If we arrest her, she might go to court. Then you'll need to testify."

"That's understood, and I would be more than pleased to assist in that. Detective, I'd like to do one more thing but I need your forensic person to go with me."

"I can arrange that," Detective Wheeler responded.

"Thanks. I want to go to the Farmington Hills park where the campers were assigned. I have a hunch I'll find the murder weapon."

"Our forensic officer is Nick Eberly. I'll give him your number."

Lou and Nick agreed to meet in the park. "Thanks for meeting with me, Nick. I've a hunch, and I need you to professionally assist me. We're looking for a knife somewhere in the back of Lot 31. If there's no knife, the suspect may have thrown it into the river behind the RV section, but I expect to find it close to Lot 31.

Lou turned the inspection of the area over to Nick after pointing at the area to be searched. Nick used a metal detector which presently gave off a signal. Nick then used tools to unearth the knife and to safely put the knife into an evidence bag.

"Is that all you need?"

"That's it. I'm sure you'll test for fingerprints on this knife. My goal was for you to find a weapon; mission accomplished. Thanks, Nick."

✂

oops
Russ was able to locate Barb Morse and he and a female officer drove to her Kalamazoo address. She willingly opened the door. Russ fully expected to see a ponytail, but her hair was short and brown. She was overweight but fashionably dressed. The moment she had feared arrived.

"Barb Morse?" Russ asked.

"Yes."

"I'm Detective Russ Wheeler of the Farmington Hills Police Department, and this is my colleague. May we come in?"

"Yes."

"We want to talk to you about your attendance at the Farmington Hills Craft Show a few weeks ago."

"I killed him. No sense running or lying. I took on evil and I won."

"We'll need to take you in. If you have an attorney, I suggest you ask him or her to meet you at police headquarters."

"Do I need to bring anything?"

"That's not necessary. Do you live alone?"

"Yes. This is upsetting. I'm afraid I'll be sick. May I go into the bathroom?"

"Sure. Officer Synk must go with you. Standard procedure."

"I really do feel sick to my stomach. I'm not going to lock the door and slit my wrists."

"Perhaps, but the moment you confessed to the murder you came under our supervision."

The two women went into the bathroom where Barb was sick. She then washed her face and entered the living room. Officer Wheeler and two officers transported her to the police station.

Chapter SEVENTEEN

Russ followed procedure, completing reports and sending copies to the prosecutor and to Judge Steven's office. Russ called Lou to inform him that Barb Morse had confessed to the murder and was in the Farmington Hills City Jail. "Looks like this case is solved, Lou."

"Good work, Russ. There are still some unanswered questions, but they may be answered in court. I will come over for the trial, but for now, I'm moving on."

Lou called Sylvia to tell her that Barb Morse had admitted to murder. "I felt certain that the killer had stayed in an RV at the park. I talked to other campers and they led me to Barb. We found the knife behind Lot 31, where her RV was assigned. I expect information about motive to come up during testimony in court. I wanted you to know what is happening before you see it on television or read it in the paper."

"Thanks, Lou. I would like to have been there, but I understand my role."

✂

Over the next couple of months, the prosecutors and defense attorneys worked on their cases, preparing for trial, sharing evidence and reports. Barb Morse was not granted bail, as she was seen as a threat to society. Trial was set for October 15.

After seating a jury and explaining the charges to them, the judge asked for opening statements from the attorneys.

The judge called upon the prosecutor for his opening statement. "Thank you, Your Honor, ladies and gentlemen of the jury. Thank you for your service in this trial. You may be sympathetic to the defendant's state of mind the night Mr. Fedewa was murdered, but we will show beyond a reasonable doubt that the defendant, Barb Morse, did kill Stan Fedewa. Murder is murder. She took a life. People get angry about things said, or states of health, or being over-drugged or not getting an addictive substance they need, but usually they do not kill others. She planned the murder. She purchased a knife for the sole purpose of killing Stan Fedewa. Do not believe that the defendant did not know what she was doing. She not only understood, she planned every step of the crime. You must find Barbara Morse guilty of murder in the first degree."

The defense attorney addressed the jury. "I am curious how many of you have heard of the 'burning bed' case in central Michigan about forty or so years ago. It was made into a movie. The outcome of that trial was that although the woman admitted she was guilty of killing her husband, she was found to be innocent by reason of insanity. The jury concluded that the murder was justified in response to the abuse inflicted on her by the victim. I suggest my client has much in common with that woman. She has admitted to killing Stan Fedewa, but she was not mentally stable when she did it. We will provide witnesses, and my client herself will explain how her mind was not clear the night she killed Mr. Fedewa. You will learn that my client was incensed when she learned Mr. Fedewa had told people falsehoods about her craft. You will learn that my client is a heroin addict. Her supply was cut off because of Mr. Fedewa. The withdrawal of that drug, combined with the false statements by Mr. Fedewa, pushed her over the edge, and she killed him. We will offer testimony to convince you beyond a reasonable doubt that my client was in a mental state where she was unable to understand the consequences of her actions."

The trial lasted five days. Each side provided a cast of experts who provided testimony on their behalf. During the trial, Barb remained emotionless. She did testify on her own behalf explaining in great detail how he was as she said, evil for what he had done or said about her and others at the craft show. During her testimony the prosecutor brought up the subject of Bulletin #7. It was introduced as evidence. With Bulletin #7 now a piece of evidence, the authorities sought its source. This led them to Becky and the phony storefront for the Middle Grove Baptist Church. The building was raided as authorities had a search warrant. There they found a file cabinet filled with bulletins of how to rob people and businesses and other suggestions for breaking the law. People associated with the organization were arrested, including Becky.

The jury deliberated for two hours and reentered the courtroom with a guilty verdict. The judge thanked jurors for their service to the citizens of Farmington Hills and dismissed them.

Barb Morse was handcuffed and led from the courtroom sobbing, showing emotion for the first time.

Lou revisited Sylvia at her home. "I want to bring you up to speed on our investigation and closure of the case."

"Thanks, Lou."

"As you know, we found Becky in Ohio. For the first time we asked the FBI for help because we were becoming involved across state lines. Our dominant suspect, Becky, was out of Michigan. With her involvement in drugs, there may have been trafficking which would come under the jurisdiction of the FBI. They located Becky and provided contact information.

"Also, I told you that I had a meeting with Georgia Myers, a vendor, who admitted she was involved but did not kill Mr. Fedewa. She, as you know, committed suicide at her Holland, Michigan, home. This led us to think we were dealing with a crafter. Because Georgia Myers told me a knife was purchased, I wanted to look for it around Barb's RV slot. I interviewed a nearby RV camper named Johnny Facely. A knife turned up behind the suspect's RV. Detective Wheeler talked with the suspect, who when confronted with the evidence, flat-out admitted she had killed Stan.

"Now, we'll move into the justice system, with trials to determine if our suspect, beyond a reasonable doubt, did murder Stan. I think you'd enjoy going with me to court on the day of the trial. It should be interesting."

"Yes, I'd like that."

"I'll let you know when it'll be. You'll need to get excused from school as it will be on a weekday. Your mom can go if she would like."

"I can't thank you enough for allowing me to learn from you," Sylvia said grinning. "You are amazing. I shall always be thankful for you and this experience. You trusted me with facts, listened to my thoughts, and guided me through the case. I'm truly blessed. Someday I hope to make you proud, for I want to follow in your footsteps."

✂

Sentencing was set for a month after the trial ended. The judge invited Barb Morse to address the court before sentencing. Holding a tear-stained paper she said, "I'm sorry the man died, but I did rid the earth of evil. I will go to jail, but many people will thank me for serving as his Karma. Yes, I did kill him. Give me a just punishment, but I beg you to have mercy."

The judge spoke briefly, "The taking of a human life is a serious crime. The jury has found you guilty of murder. I hereby sentence you to 25 years in prison, with no chance for parole." The judge then said, "Case closed." as he brought the gavel down upon the bench.

On the way out of the courtroom, Lou's cell phone vibrated. Grand Haven Chief of Police Kirk was calling.

"Yes, David. I'm just leaving the courtroom. Justice is once again served, but it was a sad situation for all involved."

"Congratulations, Lou. You must feel satisfied that the case is now history."

"A good feeling, yes."

"I'm calling because I got a call from the Montague, Michigan, Chief of Police. He's got a case there that sounds perfect for your next investigation. A murder occurred on a yacht."

"Whoa, Chief, I don't mean to cut you off, but I'm going to retire. Twenty cases and twenty books is a good place to bring to an end the excitement of man's inhumanity to man."

"Sorry to hear that, Lou, but I will call the Chief back and explain. He doesn't take 'No' for an answer, Lou. You can expect a call from him, along with an incentive. He might convince you to take on one more case."

"He can try, but I'm quite sure my days of investigating are over," Lou replied. Then two seconds later he followed with, "Oh, wait. What might his incentive be?"

"He told me he has a yacht he can't sell, and he doesn't want it anymore. He might offer it to you for next to nothing, if you take on the case."

"Hmm, a free yacht. Cruising the Great Lakes for the rest of my life. Sounds inviting."

"Does Carol like boating?" Chief Kirk asked.

"No, she's a land lubber, but she may be able to be convinced. After all, there are restaurants and shopping opportunities in every port. Am I right? What is there not to like?"

Epilogue

Becky Dawson went to prison for her role in the three crimes. She wrote Bulletin #7 which gave directions leading to two murders and one robbery.

Rod Hastings entered a rehabilitation program, stopped taking drugs, and secured a good job.

The woman who called the Tip Line hoping to claim the $5,000 reward money, learned that her tip was not related to the crime. The woman she saw had entered her own booth to retrieve some materials. Her booth was three away from Stan's booth. She was running because it was raining.

Cory Becker felt justice had been done. He knew he was the primary suspect and thanked Lou for believing him to be innocent. He returned to selling at craft shows. His business eventually regained the profitable status he had enjoyed prior to Stan Fedewa's activity.

Chelsea Porenta, the woman who was selling pens allegedly given to her by Stan, continued to sell the pens. There was nothing to link her to the killing and no way to doubt the words of Stan, and so it was assumed that Stan did give her the pens for an unknown favor.

Willie Proctor had a police record. He lived near Escanaba in the Upper Peninsula. It turns out that he did not rob the Munising vendor and that his comments to the Munising Police and to Lou were all true. The jewelry thief is still at large.

Detective Russ Wheeler was given an award for his role in solving the crime. The award was presented at a Farmington Hills council meeting. Lou and Carol were seated in the front row of the visitors section, offering Russ a standing ovation.

Sylvia Chappen turned in her project report. Lou was present for her oral report. She got an A++. And, for whatever reason, Sylvia no longer dresses the part she is playing. Why, nobody knows, but that's a behavior in the past.

Laura James, The *Grand Haven Daily Tribune* feature writer did interview Lou and Sylvia. Readers got a glimpse of Lou's compassion for others and his willingness to share his passion with a 9th grade student. Mrs. Chappen put the article and photo into a frame as a good memory for Sylvia. The article planted Detective Searing into the minds and hearts of people in his hometown. He was now a local icon and was being considered to be the Grand Marshall for next year's Coast Guard Festival Parade.

Jerry Neikirk was happy to see his vision realized and to receive an autographed copy of *Murder at the Craft Show*. He and his wife, Nancy, continue to sell his high-quality wares at shows in the Midwest.

The television show, **Dateline** used the craft show murder as a feature on their series. And even though Darlene didn't want to be involved with a television story, she was. And, she admitted to anyone who asked that she actually enjoyed it.

The **Michigan Department** responsible for sales tax licenses did determine that Stan violated tax law by not having a sales tax license and not reporting income at shows.

Jack Kelly continued to recover from his accident. Jack didn't want to press charges against those who undoubtedly caused his pain. People from Ohio no doubt were behind the threat and caused the accident near Fruitport. Jack's vanity plate (IMALSA) means I'm A Lou Searing Assistant.

Lou and Carol walked on the beach, hand in hand. Lou said out of the blue, "What would you say if I told you we could have a free yacht if I solved one more case?"

The End